The
Beltheron
Pathway

Chris Connaughton

First published in Great Britain in 2008
by
Intext Publishing

Copyright © 2008 Chris Connaughton

Names, characters and related indicia are copyright and
trademark Copyright © 2008 Chris Connaughton

Chris Connaughton has asserted his moral rights
to be identified as the author

A CIP Catalogue of this book is available from
the British Library

ISBN 978-0-9558707-0-5

Printed and bound in
Great Britain by Biddles Ltd,
King's Lynn, Norfolk

About the Author

Chris Connaughton trained as an actor and has worked in all sorts of theatres and arts centres up and down the country. He has performed as Hamlet, Romeo and Macbeth, as well as Widow Twanky, the Mad Hatter and Mr Spoon on Button Moon! His television credits include *Byker Grove, The Tide of Life, The Man Who Cried, Tales from the Piano, Call Red, Throwaways* and *Harry*.

In 1997 he set up Intext Performance to write and produce stories and plays for children. He now presents over 120 performances every year in schools throughout the UK. Chris has also performed in France, Germany, Austria, Spain, Italy, Russia, Japan and South Korea. He has written (and co-written with Paul Harman) more than 15 stories and 6 plays. *The Beltheron Pathway* is his first novel.

To order more copies of this book go to
www.thebeltheronpathway.com

DEDICATION

This book is for Lauren
who listened to my first stories
and made me want to write this one.

Acknowledgements

Many people offered their time and assistance during the writing of this book. I would like to say a huge thank you to all of them for their friendship and support. The following must be singled out for particular thanks.

Lauren Cross and Helen Field for reading a draft of the early chapters and being enthusiastic enough to make me want to continue.

All of my friends and colleagues, past and present, at CTC Theatre for helping me to find my voice and for their continuous support of my theatre work.

Ben Hendy for reading the text and giving suggestions for revisions. His ideas are always helpful, pertinent and wise.

Jean Evans for advice (and for the best digs in Darlington!)

Most of all my love and gratitude is due to Caroline for her constant support, patience and understanding and without whom many things (including this book) would not have been possible.

Prologue

The hills spread out across the far side of the valley in the dawn light. Apart from the sound of a few birds chattering there was silence; silence and stillness. Then, quietly at first, a low humming sound began. It grew in volume until the ground seemed to throb and shake. The birds stopped their singing and flew, terrified into the skies. With a flash, a tall column of brilliant white light sprang up from the ground. The light changed to a deep blood red and from out of it stepped four figures. There were two men and two women; all were dressed in plain black clothes. One of the men was holding a long, carved, golden staff in both hands. As the light began to dim around them, small bundles could be made out in the arms of the two female figures. The bundles moved every now and then, and made strange gurgling noises. The women cooed softly to comfort them after their strange journey, and rearranged the blankets to wrap them more tightly and to keep them warm in the chill morning air. More flashes of light were now appearing around this strange group, each light dropping a long black bag, or other objects and packages near by. The men quickly gathered these things together, swinging them onto their shoulders. Then, looking around to make sure that they were not leaving anything behind, the four walked quickly together across the fields towards the town. The only trace of their unusual, sudden appearance was a number of dark, round scorch marks burnt into the earth…

1

Jack's Journey

Jack Anders had grown up in London. His father, Peter and his mother, Sophie were always very busy. They ran their own business which meant that they often had to travel away from home. Sometimes Jack went with them, but he was usually looked after by a friend of his mother's; an older woman called Larena, who would stay with him while his parents were away. Larena was alright, Jack thought, but she would never let him out of her sight. She watched him like a hawk all the time. She looked a bit like a hawk as well. No, perhaps not quite like a hawk, Jack thought, more like a large raven. Her eyes were tiny and black, and her nose was long, sharp and hooked, like a raven's beak. Whenever he asked if he could do anything or go anywhere she would always come up with an excuse, or say something like: 'You are in my care now. We must stay here in the house where I can see you.' Then she would go on watching with those beady little eyes of hers.

Even his parents would be very wary of ever letting him out of their sight. But it wasn't just the usual way that his friends' families liked to make sure they knew where their children were. That only made sense, for safety's sake. He could understand that. But this was different. It was as if his mum and dad weren't just looking after him, but *guarding* him. Sometimes it made him nervous, so that he hardly dare move out of the chair where he had been told to sit quietly.

But apart from being so careful with him, most of the time it didn't seem to Jack as if his parents were interested in him at all. They would stop their conversations suddenly when he came into the room, or would be too interested in their papers or books to bother talking to him.

Jack got quite used to this as he was growing up, and there were even occasions when everything seemed to be happy. These were the times when his parents would include him in their conversations and there would be laughter in the house. This usually happened after his mother and father returned from one of their business trips. It would not last long however and soon things would be back to normal.

Now, Jack knew that no parents are ever perfect, and he was sure that, deep down, they loved him, even though he felt that they didn't *seem* to a lot of the time, or they went a very funny way about showing it.

He learnt not to expect regular treats, and even though he was allowed to invite friends over to the house, they had to sit under the watchful eyes of his mum and dad, or the dreaded Larena all the time. She would appear suddenly, as if out of nowhere, startling him and his friends so that they jumped, guiltily, even though they had not been doing anything wrong.

Soon his friends stopped wanting to come around to visit him, and made excuses. Jack knew that they were scared of Larena. Of course, no matter how politely he asked, he was not allowed to go over to visit his friends' houses at all.

So it was quite a surprise to him when one day not long after his twelfth birthday, his dad announced that Jack was going to spend three weeks with his Uncle Matt and

Auntie Jenn during the summer holidays. They lived in the town of Darlington in the north-east. Not only that, but he was going to travel on a train, *on his own*, to get there! He could hardly believe it. His dad told him that he and his mum needed to 'sort a few business things out.' Jack wasn't sure exactly what was being 'sorted out,' or why it was taking three whole weeks. His dad went on to tell him that it had to do with a big conference in Birmingham. His mum added that Larena was away on holiday with her family, so she couldn't look after him. Jack was surprised at this. He had never even known that Larena had any family.

'You'll just be bored if you come with us,' his mum said. Jack thought it was more likely that she and his dad would be bored having to put up with him in the evenings after the conference. But this thought made him feel guilty and he didn't say anything. 'And anyway,' his mother continued, 'we couldn't leave you in the hotel on your own all day.'

So that was why he was sitting on a train, heading north all on his own, without either his mum or dad, or even Larena to watch over him. *On his own*, for the first time in his life! At first this was such a novelty that it overcame any nervousness he felt.

The journey however, had been a long one. The train from London to Darlington normally took three hours. That would have been dull enough, but half way through the journey the train had stopped in the middle of the countryside for 50 minutes. This delay was long enough for Jack to stop feeling excited by his adventure, and by the time the train finally lurched into movement again he was thoroughly bored. He had finished reading the film magazine his mum had bought for him in the big newsagent's shop at the entrance to the station in London, and he was fed up of looking around him at the other passengers, trying to imagine who they were and where they were going. So, when the guard finally announced that: 'this train will shortly be arriving in Darlington' he jumped to his feet, eager to do something, *anything* other than sitting and staring out of the window. Jack pulled his rucksack onto his shoulders as the train started to slow down. He set off along the narrow aisle in between the rows of seats, in search of his small suitcase, which he had stuffed into the luggage rack at the end of the carriage. He wobbled from side to side as the train lurched. As he pulled his case out, he tripped and bumped into a large bearded man who was also struggling with his own bags. The man turned and stared at him with angry, yellowy-green eyes. He wore a long black coat that hung down like a cloak. Jack murmured 'sorry sir' in a low, embarrassed voice, and hurried past.

The boredom of the journey changed quickly to anxiety as the long platform of Darlington station began to rush past. This was the town where his aunt, uncle and cousin Helen lived. It had been over two years since his mum and dad had last brought him up here for a visit; just before he had turned ten. That time they had all travelled together in his dad's car. It had been one of the good times, and he remembered playing guessing games in the back, mum shouting out clues, and dad laughing and telling them both stories as they drove north. It was very different this time, travelling on his own. Jack had been so protected all the time he was growing up, that he always felt shy and nervous with people he didn't know very well. He didn't *want* to spend his precious holidays so far away, with an aunt, uncle and cousin he could hardly even remember. Even staying at home – with Larena watching his every move – would be better than that. He started to wonder if they would even be there

6

at the station to welcome him. His mum had said that he would be fine, the guard on the train had been told to keep an eye on him, and that Jenn, Matt and Helen would be there as soon as he stepped off the train. But would they recognise him? What was his cousin Helen like now?

The train made a final jerk forwards, and stopped. Several other people were also getting off, and when Jack stepped onto the platform he had to wait until the crowds had thinned a bit before looking around for his relatives.

'Jack? Jack! Over here!'

He turned around and saw them standing a little way off, by a large Arrivals/Departures notice board. It was Auntie Jenn who had called out to him. Now she started waving and walking towards him. Helen and Uncle Matt followed just behind, with smiles on their faces. The two adults looked just about the same as he remembered; Auntie Jenn with lots of curling, bouncy, light brown hair and big, happy light green eyes; Uncle Matt very tall and thin, with a toothy grin that seemed to be too wide to fit on his narrow face. Helen, however, looked very different to what he remembered. She and Jack were about the same age, he just over twelve, and she eleven and three quarters. The last time they had met, she had appeared to be much younger than him, but now somehow, Jack thought she seemed very confident, as if she was far *older* than he was. She was even a little bit taller than him now. 'But at least they seem happy enough to see me,' he said to himself, and a little of his nervousness slipped away from him. In another moment he was being kissed by Auntie Jenn, and Uncle Matt had his hand firmly on his shoulder, saying, 'Good to see you, how was the journey? You haven't half grown. Hasn't he shot up, Jenn?'

Jack was embarrassed at their attention on the platform which was still crowded. He wasn't used to being shown such affection and being kissed – certainly not in public. If his parents hadn't thought he needed a kiss when he was little then he definitely didn't need one now! He was twelve for goodness sake! Helen was grinning at him. He stuck his chin down onto his chest, trying not to catch his cousin's eyes too much as he muttered hello. She wasn't laughing at his embarrassment though, just smiling happily at him. In fact, none of them seemed to notice his shyness, and they carried on talking – almost non-stop, it seemed to Jack.

'It must have been a bit borin' on there all that time, eh Jack?'

'Train's nearly an hour late! What was the delay about, did they say?'

'I bet you're hungry.'

'Mum's got a smashin' meal planned for tonight – I hope you like pasta!'

His uncle took his bags from him and the four of them set off towards the station car park. They passed the taxi rank where Jack noticed the large bearded man he had bumped into on the train. The man was struggling to get a long bulky package into the boot of one of the taxis. The package looked as if it might have fishing rods or golf clubs in it, thought Jack. The big man had already knocked off the taxi driver's cap with the end of the package. He was just bending down to pick it up, when the package poked the driver in the eye. Jack couldn't help laughing out loud as he walked past. The man stood up to his full height and glared at him with those yellowy-green eyes. The look seemed to freeze Jack's laugh in his throat, and made him cough as if he had swallowed something too quickly. He turned and hurried away, following Helen and the others to their car. They all bundled in, still chattering away. None of them seemed to worry too much whether Jack responded to their comments and questions or not. To Jack, Helen and her mum and dad were the epitome of the happy, relaxed family.

Soon they had pulled out of the station. They began to make their way through the busy tea-time traffic onto the Yarm Road which led out of the east side of the town. The happy chattering continued all the time. Eventually Jack started to relax more and joined in with the conversation.

'Thanks very much for coming to pick me up.'

'No problem Jack,' replied his aunt, 'we've bin lookin' forward to seein' you again.'

'How's your mum and dad?' added Uncle Matt, 'have they managed to get rid of…'

'Let's not worry about all that now Matty' interrupted Jenn, quickly. 'I'm sure they're fine, aren't they love?'

Jack didn't reply. He wasn't sure what Uncle Matt and Aunty Jenn were talking about. It must be something to do with his parents' business. It sounded to Jack as if his aunt and uncle expected him to know a lot more about things at home than he actually did. Now that he thought about it, recently his parents *had* seemed a bit more distracted than usual. Not worried particularly, just as if their thoughts were somewhere else. They were obviously concerned about all of the things that they had to prepare before the big conference in Birmingham. But as usual they hadn't mentioned anything to him. They hardly ever spoke about their work while he was around. Why should they? They didn't talk to him about anything much. He stared out of the window of the car for a few minutes in silence, caught up with his own thoughts. He didn't even catch the whispered conversation in the front seats as Jenn told Matt to 'think before opening your big mouth! Remember, he doesn't know *anything* yet.'

Soon they were well out of the town and driving along a country road, which ran alongside the runway of a small airport. 'We took off from there on our 'olidays last year' chirped Helen. After another fifteen minutes or so, Uncle Matt flicked the left indicator and turned off the main road and onto a single-track lane bordered by two high hedges. Now they really felt to be heading into the open countryside. The late afternoon sun was dipping lower in the sky now and casting long shadows across the fields which Jack glimpsed every now and then as the car passed a fence or a gap in the hedge. After another mile or so they came to a small village, with two long rows of cottages that ran around either side of a wide village green, complete with a pond in the middle.

'Better than dirty old London I bet, eh?' smirked Helen. The words could easily have been taken as an insult, or meant to hurt, but when he looked at his cousin she was still smiling. Her face was friendly and open. She seemed excited to introduce him to where she lived and to be able to share it with him.

'Look over there,' she continued; 'we've got ducks on the pond and everything.'

Sure enough, there were several ducks splashing about at the side of the water. It looked beautiful. Even so, Jack wasn't sure he agreed with her about it being better than London. He wasn't going to admit that it was better than the big, exciting city where he lived, but it *did* look much more interesting than he had hoped. When Jack had last visited them, his relatives had lived in the town of Darlington itself, in a Victorian terraced house close to the supermarket. He hadn't thought much of the town that time. This though, was a different thing entirely. There were two big trees which stood at one edge of the pond and Jack thought that they looked like great climbers. There was space in the middle branches for a lookout post over the whole village. He had always wanted to climb trees, but at home he was never allowed to. As he looked at the trees a large raven flew down and settled on the topmost branch. It obviously frightened the other smaller birds as several of them, mainly sparrows from what he could make out, scattered immediately into the air.

'Hah! It looks like Larena!' Jack thought to himself. Being able to make fun of his childminder at a safe distance, with the knowledge he didn't have to see her again for weeks and weeks cheered him up even more. He looked back at the bird again and stuck his tongue out at it. The raven sat there, gazing around impassively. Jack grinned.

Helen tapped the car window with her finger. He turned from watching the birds to look in the direction that she was pointing. 'That's our house. There, that one at the end of the green' she said.

Jack looked out in the direction she had just pointed. Set some way back from the road was a large, stone house. There was a porch at the front covered with a long climbing ivy, and at one side of the house was a huge garage. 'This bit used to be the stables,' said Uncle Matt as he drove the car towards the double doors of the garage.

The house really was beautiful but suddenly Jack felt afraid. A strange anxiety welled up in his chest. He couldn't explain the feeling, even to himself, but as the car stopped and he glanced through the car window, he got the sensation that someone inside was watching him!

'Is...is there anyone else at home?' he asked in a low voice.

'It'll just be the four of us Jack' Aunty Jenn replied. She made her way to the front porch door fumbling for her keys. Jack held back, hovering by the car. Helen was already following her mum up the path. Dusk was all around them now and the low sun in the deep red sky lit up the sandy coloured walls and reflected on the big windows. The reflected sunlight looked like a raging fire inside the house. The feeling of dread in Jack's mind wouldn't go away. He had never felt anything like this before. It was like a dream where you know something terrible is around the corner, but you can't do anything to stop it. He looked once again at the crimson sunset's reflection in the windows. Was it just his imagination that made the red glow seem like fire….or blood? No. Not just his imagination. Something *was* wrong, he knew it. He wanted to cry out; 'don't go in there' and he felt the words forming in his mouth ready to scream: 'there's evil, evil in the house! Don't go in!' but he couldn't make a sound. Suddenly, everything seemed to go black.

The next thing Jack knew, Helen was standing over him, looking down with a worried expression on her face. For some reason he was lying on the floor. He heard a thump on the gravel of the driveway as Uncle Matt dropped Jack's rucksack and the bags that he had been lifting from the car boot and came running towards them.

'Give him a bit o' space Helen love. Must be the journey. Poor lad must be shattered. 'Ere, move over, let's get at him.'

Jack felt himself being lifted up and carried inside, past Auntie Jenn who was holding the door open for them. Just before they went in, he looked towards the windows once more, but in the last few moments the sun had finally dipped down below the horizon, and the fiery glow could no longer be seen. The house looked perfectly normal again and Jack shook his head to clear his mind as they crossed the threshold into the hallway.

There had been such confusion and concern over Jack that none of them had noticed the taxi driving slowly past on the opposite side of the village green. They did not see the face that peered at them out of the rear window of the taxi, the bearded face of a large man with yellowy-green eyes. The only thing that might have seen him was the large raven at the top of the tree, but the bird didn't seem to take any notice. It flapped its wings and took off, circling the pond lazily a couple of times before flying off over the roof of Matt, Jenn and Helen's house.

2

A Warm Welcome

Inside the house, Jack was taken straight upstairs to the guest room. Matt sat him down on the bed and Jenn walked to the window to open it and let in some fresh evening air. After a few moments, Helen came rushing in with a glass of water. Jack took it and thanked her. He reassured the others that he was already feeling alright, even though he could still feel his heart hammering away in his chest as if he had just finished the main race at sports day. They left him to start his unpacking.

Alone, Jack walked over to the open window. He breathed in the cool breeze and gazed out over the darkening fields. They stretched away from the back of the house to a view of the Cleveland Hills, some ten or fifteen miles away to the East. He focused on the hills for a few minutes; breathing steadily and feeling his heart begin to slow down to its normal pace. He noticed that one of the hills had a sharp, angled summit which curved around at a strange angle. It reminded him of a picture of a witch's hat from one of his storybooks when he was younger.

As he looked out, lost in his thoughts, there was a knock on the door and Helen's face peered around it.

'Can I come in?'

'Help yourself.' Jack was glad to see her. She seemed genuinely kind, and concerned about him.

'You feeling better?'

He nodded. 'Much better. Thanks.' He hesitated. 'Feel a bit stupid though.'

'Don't worry. It can happen to anyone. Especially when…' she seemed to stop herself, as if she had changed her mind about something she had been about to say. After a brief moment she continued in a slightly different, more offhand way, '…when you've had a long journey.'

'I think I'll like it here,' Jack went on, eager to change the subject. He pointed out of the window. 'Can you get up onto those hills?'

'Oh yes. You often see walkers out there. It's a bit of a climb though.'

'I don't mind that.'

'I'll ask Dad. There might be a chance of getting up there for a day. Take some sandwiches.'

'I like the look of that hill there.' Jack went on, pointing at the strange shape he had noticed a minute before. 'It looks as if it should be called Mount Witchcap, or something.'

'Nothing so dramatic, I'm afraid.' Helen answered with a grin. 'It's called Roseberry Topping. More like a pudding than a spooky witch's meeting place!'

They laughed and continued chatting easily for a while about exploring the fields and lanes nearby. Before long they had started to plan a trip to the next village, where some of Helen's friends owned horses. Jack's face fell.

'I'm afraid I don't know how to ride.' He said. 'There's not much chance, living in London. I don't know if I'd be any good.'

'Don't worry about that. My friend Mel's got a quiet, easygoing pony called Jigsaw. It's almost impossible to fall off him.'

'I might give it a go.' Jack still sounded unconvinced. He didn't want to show himself up in front of Helen, or any of her friends that he hadn't even met yet.

'I can teach you anyway.' Helen continued, still full of enthusiasm. 'I've been on and off horses since before I could walk. And if you're still not sure, there are bikes that you can ride to keep up. You do ride a bike don't you?'

Jack was just saying, oh yes he loved bikes, he was great on a bike, when Helen saw the film magazine sticking out of his rucksack. She picked it up and started leafing through the pages.

'You like going to the cinema?'

'Love it! I go a lot in London, and I've got loads of DVDs.' The truth was that films were an escape for him. He could enjoy hours on his own watching them on TV when Larena was in the house, and she wouldn't bother him at all.

'There's a decent cinema in Darlington.' Helen suggested, 'and a big multi-screen nearby in Middlesbrough. We could go one day if the weather's rubbish.'

Jack was happily agreeing to this when Aunty Jenn called up the stairs to say that dinner was ready. Helen threw the magazine back onto the bed and raced out of the room. 'Come on!'

Jack realised that he was very hungry and he rushed downstairs after his cousin, meaning to give dinner his full attention.

The family gathered around a huge old wooden table in the middle of the kitchen. His uncle pointed Jack to the big chair at one end of the table. 'You're our guest of honour this evening Jack' joked Uncle Matt. 'Special place over there. Head of the table.'

Helen walked around the table, pouring fruit juice out of a tall glass jug into tumblers for all of them. Auntie Jenn placed a colourful serving bowl on the table filled with steaming hot ribbons of green, yellow and red pasta. Next she brought a wide dish of tomato and cheese sauce from the oven and began spooning it over the pasta. There were platefuls of warm bread with sweet-smelling sultanas and pine nuts baked in them, and an exotic looking salad with oranges and what appeared to be flower petals in amongst the green. 'You can eat those flowers, you know,' chirped Helen. 'They're all edible.' Jack's nose wrinkled in delight at the delicious aroma, which filled the warm room.

'Hope you've got a big appetite.'

'Looks lovely Auntie Jenn. Thanks very much.'

He was feeling better by the minute. Not only had he recovered from his earlier faint, but his worries about what this visit might be like, and his doubts about his relatives, had almost entirely faded away. They were all so nice to him and made him feel so welcome. Even the image in his head of the red, fiery windows and the accompanying dread he had felt when he fainted had sunk down into the back of his mind. Now he just felt the remains of his embarrassment at showing himself up. But that too began to fade away. He didn't even give it another thought as he tucked into his food. A warm glow welled up inside him and he looked around happily.

'This is great, thank you very much.'

'Look at him put it away!'

'I told you he'd be hungry.'

'And I thought our Helen could eat.'

Their plates were soon emptied. Dessert followed, and Jack was delighted to see that it was an enormous bowl of trifle – his favourite. Layers and layers of jelly, soaked sponge, cream and multi-coloured fruit, with chocolate flakes crumbled onto the top. Things were just getting better and better.

After dinner, when they had all collapsed into armchairs or onto the long, cosy green sofa in the living room, Auntie Jenn said; 'you'd better ring home Jack. Let them know that you're here safe and sound.'

Jack felt a little guilty. He had been there for nearly three hours and he had forgotten to call. He had promised his mum on the platform at King's Cross that he would give them a ring as soon as he had arrived. His fainting fit outside the house and all the fuss that had been made of him, followed by that superb tea, had pushed it clean out of his mind. What's more, his mum had been particularly insistent that he ring. 'You won't forget now will you?' Then she had hugged him very tight, which felt really strange, she hardly ever did anything like that. His dad had seemed distracted – as usual – and he kept looking all around him, quite nervously Jack thought, as if he expected to see someone that he would prefer not to.

Helen showed Jack into the hall where the telephone was, and then left him alone while he dialled. He was glad to be on his own to make his call, and he realised how kind it had been of Helen to think about it, and give him his privacy. He listened to the sound of the phone ringing at the other end, and pictured it sitting on the hall table at home. He imagined his mum or dad rushing to pick up the receiver. The phone kept on ringing. Surely they had heard it by now? Jack let it ring three, four, five more times before hanging up and trying again. 'Must have got the wrong number' he thought. 'They weren't going anywhere tonight, they said so. They said they would stay in.' The phone continued to ring. No answer. He let it go on for two whole minutes this time, counting them out by the second hand on the wall clock in his aunt and uncle's hallway. Still no answer. He dialled a third time, carefully, making absolutely sure of his number. The phone must have been on its twentieth ring when Auntie Jenn came out into the hall. 'Everything ok?' she mouthed silently to him.

Jack shook his head and hung up.

'They're not in.'

'You sure love?'

'I let it ring for ages. I dialled three times'

A strange, worried look came over Jenn's face for a moment. Then she smiled at him. 'Don't worry pet, they must have popped out. Maybe gone for a nice meal, or to the local for a drink? They don't have to think about a babysit… sorry, a child minder while you're up here do they?'

'No. They were going to stay in. They said they would, at least until I had called.'

Auntie Jenn's worried expression came back but she disguised it – not very successfully Jack thought.

'Try their mobile.' She suggested.

Jack did so, but just got the answering service. He dialled three more times before giving up.

''It is a bit late now Jack love. Look its half past nine. They probably gave up waiting and just decided to go out. Must have forgotten to switch the mobile on. We'll try them again first thing in the morning.'

But this was wrong. Jack and Auntie Jenn both knew it was, even if they weren't admitting it to each other. His mum and dad would have called before they went out, to make sure he was there, and safe. They, of all people would want to know where he was. Something was wrong. Jack knew it. But what?

3
Under Attack

He found it hard to get to sleep that night. The strange bed didn't seem to want him to get comfortable, and all the time he was thinking about home. Where had Mum and Dad gone? Uncle Matt had tried to ring them once more before Jack had come up to bed, and then checked the number with the operator, but without success. There had to be an innocent, easy explanation, he kept telling himself. But he tossed and turned, unable to switch off his mind and relax.

It must have been well after midnight, and finally his thoughts had begun to wander off into sleep, when he heard the murmuring of voices in the room below him. Instantly he was wide awake again, his eyes open and staring at the ceiling. Very quietly he turned back the bedclothes and swung his legs out. Putting his feet gingerly on to the floor he slowly moved towards his bedroom door. Creeping through into the upstairs hallway he made his way to the top of the staircase. The stairs were wide enough for two people to pass each other without difficulty, and there was a turning and a small landing area half way down with a bookcase and pots and vases on a couple of stands.

The low voices which had disturbed him were still talking as he crept to the turning in the staircase. Three voices. Uncle Matt, Auntie Jenn, and another, strong voice which he didn't recognise. Moving slowly and carefully, so as not to make a sound, he leant forward to try to catch the words. What he heard didn't make any sense, but still carried a feeling of dread to his heart.

'…must be an explanation for why they didn't answer the phone.' Uncle Matt was saying. The strange, deeper voice answered him.

'I hope there *is* a simple explanation. Even so, we cannot take any chances. I'll send a Pulver to check up first thing in the morning.'

'Peter acted quickly to get the boy out; the Rish can't have suspected anything.'

This made Jack jump. He gave a gasp which he was sure could have been heard downstairs. Peter was his dad's name. *'Peter acted quickly to get the boy out.'* They were talking about him! Him and his dad! But what was a *Pulver?* And what did *Rish* mean? All of the dread he had felt earlier came rushing back to Jack now as he continued to listen to the conversation below.

'…been weeks setting this thing up,' this was Auntie Jenn's voice, 'if there *is* a traitor, he has had plenty of time to inform the Rish that we meant to get Jack away to safety.'

'But *is* he safe?' This was the strange voice again. 'Should we not move him on elsewhere? After all, if the Rish *do* have Peter and Sophie they may be tortured to tell of his whereabouts. We cannot take any risk with the boy.'

Jack gave a whimper of fear from his hiding place on the stairs and shrank even further back into the shadows. Just behind where he had been crouching, next to the bookcase in the turn of the stairway, there was a small three-legged table. A large vase sat on top of it. As he moved back, Jack's elbow brushed against the vase and it toppled from the stand. Jack gasped and reached out both arms to try to catch it. But he was too late. The vase dropped onto the floor with a loud crash.

The voices downstairs stopped immediately. There was a second of absolute silence, and then a voice downstairs, the one Jack didn't recognise, called out; 'They're here! The Rish! It is all too late!' An uproar of sound and commotion began below him.

Before he could even stand up and run back upstairs, footsteps had crossed the hallway and a cloaked figure, the tallest and thinnest person that Jack had ever seen, came bounding up towards him, three steps at a time. Jack cowered backwards, terrified. The figure caught him up in his arms and cradled him in his pale blue cloak. He looked all around, and then his gaze fell to the ground at their feet. He saw the broken vase.

'The noise, the crash. That was you?'

Jack stammered an apologetic reply; 'I'm s...sorry. I, I...didn't mean to...'

Matt and Jenn were now halfway up the stairs. The tall figure placed Jack back on his feet, where he wobbled unsteadily, as if someone had replaced his bones with spaghetti. Then the stranger turned and spoke to all three of them.

'I apologise for my panic. The boy is fine. The Rish are not here.'

'Thank heavens' Auntie Jenn murmured. She had gone very pale, Jack noticed. Her green eyes were darting nervously around, and Uncle Matt put a hand on her shoulder to comfort her, although he looked just as unsettled as she did.

'What's going on?' This came from Helen who was standing on the landing above them. Then she did something which made all the recent madness and confusion even more impossible for Jack to understand. With a cry of: 'Ohh, *Parenon*, thank goodness it's you!' she ran down the now very crowded staircase, past Jack, and flung her arms around the tall figure's waist (which was about as high as it was possible for her to reach).

Now it was Jack's turn to say, 'What's going on?' The tension and uncertainty of the last few hours, and the feeling that everyone else knew things that he was completely in the dark about, made a strange, tight twisting in his chest. Jack realised that he was feeling very upset. He even felt tears of frustration welling up in his eyes. Who on earth was this new arrival?

Helen stopped hugging the tall stranger and took Jack by the hand. 'Come on,' she whispered to him, 'it's alright.' They all started to go back downstairs into the kitchen.

'It's high time you were told,' said Uncle Matt firmly, when they had all settled themselves back around the kitchen table. The blue-cloaked stranger occupied the top seat, where Jack had sat for dinner. Uncle Matt turned to his wife and continued; 'I've said so since he was little. He should have been told long before now. After all, we told our Helen, and she's been fine. She's had chance to get used to what it all means, learn some of the tricks an' all that. Prepare herself for what's to come.'

'He must be told now.' Parenon spoke in a high, clear voice. 'The Rish are growing bolder all the time – the disappearance of Jack's parents is proof of that." Parenon turned towards Jack and now it seemed that there was a kindly gleam deep in his eyes as he spoke. "We have held our tongues in this matter with due respect for your mother and father's wishes.' He paused just for a moment, before pacing his hand firmly on Jack's shoulder and continuing in a lower tone. 'Now we must tell you of your history – your *true* history. You do not know it Jack, but you have gifts, special skills, which have a tremendous importance in our battle against the evil ones.'

'Evil ones?'

'The Rish, those of whom you heard me speak before. They are the servants of one who holds immense power and they are close to gaining victory in our present struggle.' Parenon paused briefly and glanced around at the others. 'Helen here has already begun to learn about her skills, and how to marshal her talents. She knows the secrets of her birth, her place in the struggle. You, as yet, do not.'

Jack looked from one to the other of them around the table as if they were mad. 'Is this a joke?' he began. 'Because if it is, I don't think that it's very f...' His voice tailed off as he looked up at the man they called Parenon. Something in the strangeness of his clothes and the intensity of his gaze made him believe that it wasn't a joke at all. 'Then it must be a dream,' he reassured himself. 'Hardly surprising after the day I've had.'

His aunt touched him gently on the shoulder. 'We should have told you before my dear,' she began. 'We understand that now. But it was so hard for any of us to know where to start, or how you would react you see. We had no way of knowing whether you would even believe us.' She smiled, 'and obviously, you don't!'

Uncle Matt interrupted. 'We must start at the beginning, Jenn.' He turned towards Jack; 'this goes back a long way Jack. A long way into history.'

He paused and looked back at Jenn, then continued. 'It's so difficult; you have to forget about all you know of the world. You will have to think about things in a completely different way.' He took a deep breath. 'There are two *other* worlds, ones that exist behind this one, or rather, alongside it. What happens in one world can influence what goes on in the other two and ....' His Uncle's voice drifted off as he saw the bemused expression on his nephew's face. 'Sorry. This isn't making any sense to you.'

'And why should it?' Interrupted Auntie Jenn. 'What

your Uncle is trying to say is that one of the other worlds, the one that our family is linked to, is…'

Jenn's next words were drowned out by a long, drawn out wail from outside. It sounded like the call of a huge seagull – but this sound went on and on without stopping, Helen stiffened and reached out to grip Jack's hand. Uncle Matt and Auntie Jenn looked at each other hurriedly, as if unable to decide what to do.

Parenon was already on his feet. He had leapt up so swiftly that he was by the window – peering through the narrow gap in the curtains – before Jack had time to think. One of Parenon's hands was on the curtain; the other had dropped inside his cloak where it grasped the bright hilt of a long sword. The keening, wailing sound outside continued, and grew louder. 'You must go,' shouted Parenon, 'I will deal with these as best I can.'

The others all paused, still uncertain as to what action to take. 'Do as I say!' Parenon's voice was now harsh and brief. 'Take the children upstairs. Go now!' He didn't turn to look at them. His eyes were fixed on what was outside the window. Parenon began to draw the long sword out of its scabbard. Even in the haste and turmoil, Jack noticed the glint of ornate silver and jewels around the pommel of the handle, and the thick, dark leather straps that held the scabbard to Parenon's belt.

Matt grabbed Jack by the elbow and hauled him to his feet. 'Explanations'll have to wait, come on!' The four of them hurried to the foot of the staircase. Helen was in the lead, and was the first to begin to climb the steps when there was a crash behind them. Turning around, Jack saw that one of the kitchen windows had shattered and a long snaking arm was winding around the frame. Parenon leapt towards it, his bright blade flashing. It struck the arm and with a bone-shivering scream it was pulled sharply outside again.

'Go!' yelled Parenon. 'I cannot hold them forever!'

Once more they began to climb the stairs. Helen was still surging on ahead when suddenly all the lights went out. They were plunged into darkness. At the same instant the screams and wails from outside multiplied in volume. It felt to Jack as if someone were pressing the palms of their hands hard against the sides of his head. He shook his head to try to release the pressure but it was no use. Then there was a strong hand on his back, pushing him forwards. He tripped, but immediately felt another, smaller hand in his, in front of him, pulling him on. It was Helen. 'Follow me!' she screamed in his ear. He crashed onwards, catching his toe hard against the rise of the steps. Up and up he stumbled after his cousin, around the corner of the landing. On, in total darkness, not remembering in his panic where he was in this house which was still so new and unfamiliar to him. He trusted completely in the hand that still gripped his; leading him away from the dreadful noises below. Parenon's voice was now mingled with the screams in a loud battle cry; 'For Mage and Council!' and the clang of metal on metal rang out clearly. Suddenly he was pulled forwards through a doorway and heard it slam closed behind him. Jack felt Helen's breath close to his ear and a whispered: 'stay still and quiet. I know what to do to stay hidden.'

She left him for a minute, standing alone in the blackness. Fainter sounds of battle still raged from the downstairs rooms. He heard Helen speak a single word from across the room. It sounded to Jack something like 'Illumen' and a dim greenish light began to spread out from something Helen was now holding. The light continued to grow until it filled the room. Then she was with him again, slipping a small bottle into the pocket of her dressing-gown, and pushing a hard, round object about the size of an orange in between his hands. It was this object that was giving off the greenish light. Her fingers pressed down tightly onto his own. The green glow began to filter through their fingers from the ball shape, criss-crossing the room with shafts of light

'What *is* that thing?' asked Jack.

'Ssh. No time to explain.'

'But…'

'Sshh!'

Jack had to be content to forget the numerous questions which were swimming around and around in his mind. He turned his attention back to the glowing ball in their joined hands.

'Take a deep breath.' Helen told him. He did as he was told and took a long breath in. 'Now let it out slowly at the same time as me.'

Helen took a breath herself and then nodded to him. Jack followed her instructions, blowing a thin stream of air through his lips. He felt himself deflating, growing weaker as he ran out of air. Helen's expression told him to keep going. Her eyes were fixed directly into his but she was starting to shake as her own breath ran out.

'Bit more…jus' a bit more…' she groaned through her clenched teeth.' That's it, NOW!'

As she shouted the last word she threw the glowing ball into the air. Jack stared at it, mesmerised. Instead of falling back down towards them it hovered in the air about six inches above their heads, rotating slowly, and filling the whole room with light. This was different to normal light though, Jack thought. It seemed to cling to them, and he could feel it, like a solid thing all around him. He felt strangely comforted by it, as if someone had thrown a blanket over him to keep him warm in a cold room. This strange sensation lasted for about thirty seconds, before the light began to dim again, and the ball descended into the palm of Helen's outstretched hand. Jack tore his gaze away from it, even though he was still fascinated by the beautiful, mysterious thing, and he looked back into Helen's eyes.

Helen returned his gaze. In spite of everything, the fear, her worry about what might be happening downstairs to her mum and dad, and the strange Parenon, she smiled.

'You poor thing. You look so...so...what's the word? Bemused! I'll try to let you in on this bit by bit.' She paused, as if wondering where to begin her explanation. 'What we've just done is called sidestepping. And it wasn't a bad try to say you've never done it before.'

'Sidestepping?' Jack repeated.

'Yes, it's a good trick when you've learnt it properly. Only odd-number generations of the Select can do it. You know, third, fifth, seventh generation, and so on. And even then you need to have another person with you. You have to work together with the Kron to manage it properly.'

'Is that the Kron?' asked Jack, pointing down to the ball.

'Yes, that's right.' It had almost stopped glowing now. 'Anyway, you and I are twenty-third generation. An odd number, see? The even numbers, like your mum and dad, and my parents, they have different skills.'

'Wait, wait!' pleaded Jack, who was so confused that he thought he may be near to tears again. He could feel them brimming up behind his eyes through a mixture of terror and frustration. He sniffed loudly and brushed his hand across his face before looking up at her again. Helen was gazing at him closely, an expression of concern in her eyes.

Jack sniffed again. 'I'm sorry. I know I'm being

really thick, but I just don't understand any of this. I can't figure out anything that's happened to me since I got here. And what was all that about just now, with that flying ball thing? The, the…Kron? And what's happened downstairs? It's gone so quiet all of a sudden.'

'Yes.' Replied Helen, moving away from him and tip-toeing towards the door. 'It has gone quiet. We should be all right now. We're not there any more you see.'

'Not there? What do you mean, not there?'

'Well, I suppose I mean we're not *here*.'

Jack shook his head, his mouth hanging open. 'Not here? You're daft. Where are we then?'

Helen continued, 'Well we're still upstairs in the house, but for a while we sort of – dodged sideways. We were halfway between being in this room, with all that still going on downstairs, and halfway to not being anywhere at all. You see? Sidestepping'

Jack didn't see at all. He shook his head again. It must be the shock, he thought. All this excitement's made her go bonkers.

'We can probably go back downstairs again now.'

'Down there?'

Now it was Helen's turn to shake her head at him.

'It's alright. It's like I just said, we sidestepped.'

Her certainty comforted him a bit. He had to trust her, he realised.

'So have things stopped down there now? Did your sidestepping stop what was going on?'

Helen paused and looked down at the Kron for a moment. 'No. Sidestepping doesn't change anything that's already happened around you. It can't alter other people's actions. But it takes you away from it for a while. So you can't be hurt by it.' She grinned broadly; 'it was great for playing hide and seek with all the other kids in the park in

Darlington when I was little. Mum used to help me, just to see the look on the other kids' faces.'

'You've known how to do this since you were *little*?'

'For years and years. It was one of the first things Dad taught me.'

Jack had a sudden pang of jealousy. He couldn't imagine his own dad ever taking the time to teach him anything like that.

'And are you sure you think it's safe to go down now?' He repeated.

Helen had placed the Kron back in a drawer, closed it and was half way through the bedroom door. 'Yes, come on.'

Still shaking his head in disbelief, Jack followed her down the hallway.

4

The Pathway

They made their way down the staircase and back into the kitchen. The sight that met their eyes stopped them in their tracks. Their mouths hung open as they stared around at the devastation.

The large, oak kitchen door had been split down the middle. It lay in two pieces on the floor. The windows were shattered and the curtains hung in ribbons from the bent and buckled poles. Something – or things – with tremendous power and force had burst in, and the signs of the battle, which they had heard from upstairs, were clearly visible all around them. The heavy kitchen table was turned over onto one side and three deep, uneven scratches had been scored down the entire length, as if by knives, or vicious talons. Crockery, pots and pans were scattered around the room, mostly smashed into hundreds of pieces, or twisted beyond repair. Jack noticed something hanging onto the corner of a smashed chair. He bent down and picked it up. It was a small, torn fragment of pale blue cloth.

'Parenon's cloak,' he murmured in a low voice. Helen nodded. She gulped as she saw the smears of red which ran down from one corner of the table and onto the floor. Jack followed the direction of her eyes.

'Blood?' he asked.

Helen nodded again, slowly. Stepping towards him she took the blue cloth from his fingers and held it up in front of her. Muttering under her breath, she clenched the fabric tight in her left hand, and reached into her pocket for the tiny jar which she had put there earlier, just before they had used the Kron. 'Here's another trick for you,' she said to Jack. 'I think I even prefer this to sidestepping.' A note of pride entered her voice. 'I'm the only one I know of who can do it.' They had both been talking in low voices since coming back down into the kitchen and now Helen's grew even quieter as she continued, as if she hardly even wanted to hear herself. Jack had to lean forward to catch her words. 'If I take this piece of Parenon's cloak and sprinkle just a few drops of this liquid onto it, we should be able to see where he has gone. Then I might even be able to create a way to get to him.'

Placing the scrap of cloak onto the floor, she unscrewed the bottle lid and shook it for a moment, so that tiny sparks flew out. They drifted slowly down onto the small patch of blue cloth and, with a sudden crackling sound, a white column of light shot up towards the ceiling. At the same time a low humming sound filled the room.

'Fantastic!' shouted Helen, 'it's starting to work!'

Poor Jack could only stand back amazed as Helen stepped forwards into the column of light. He held his breath and could feel his heart hammering loud and quick in his chest. As soon as both of Helen's feet were planted firmly in the pool of brightness on the floor, the humming began to grow louder and the tone changed. Until that moment it had been a low murmur, so low that they could hardly hear it. Now it was as if someone were turning the dials on a radio – the volume going up and the frequency changing to a higher pitch. Helen turned around. 'This doesn't seem right,' she said above the humming sound. 'This feels different to the last time I tried. When I stand here, I should be able to see where Parenon has gone and

….Ouch!'

She flinched as if someone had struck her.

'Get out of there.' Replied Jack in a panicked voice. 'Come back over here.' He held out his hand and stepped forwards towards her. At that moment the light grew brighter, turned deep red and started to pulse. Jack shielded his eyes with the back of his other hand. He could still see Helen, but the red light was so vivid that she had become blurred. Jack could just make her out as she turned around to face him. Helen smiled and it seemed to Jack that she was about to step back towards him – and safety – when the humming sound suddenly stopped. The bright red pulsing light gave a flash outwards, filling the whole room for an instant and engulfing Jack, so that even with his hand raised to his eyes he was blinded.

He took a deep breath and peered out through his fingers again. His vision began to come back in mad swirls of colour and sparks. Jack blinked twice, and then he shook his head to clear it. He looked around him. All that was left in the room was the pale column of white light, but even that was now beginning to fade. And that was all. Helen had vanished.

Jack spun around. 'Helen? Helen!'

There was no reply. His voice rose as he called out again; 'Helen? Where are you?' Still no reply. Feeling the panic start to rise up in him he raced towards the door. He shouted out for her once more. Silence. He was now completely alone. He had to get out of the house, try to find someone to help him. Could things get any worse he wondered?

Just then he realised that they could; things could get much worse. Because he was *not* alone! Even as he ran towards the open doorway, a figure had stepped into it. It was the figure of a large man with a beard and bright, yellowy green eyes.

Jack stared up at the man for a few moments. His head was still spinning, but now with questions as well as fear. Surely this was the man he had bumped into on the train, and then seen at the taxi rank at the station? What was he doing here? In this house? Jack's fear took over again. He began to step backwards, back to the centre of the kitchen and the dim column of light which had now all but disappeared. He cowered away from the strange burly man, too scared to take his eyes from him. He bumped up against the kitchen wall and began feeling along it with one hand as he continued to move away from the huge figure.

'Wait!' the man's voice was deep and commanding. In spite of himself, Jack felt he had no choice but to listen.

'I know how confused and afraid you must be feeling. But please do not try to run from me. Let me try to explain what is happening'

'Who are you?' screamed Jack, terror overwhelming him now as the night seemed to take yet another turn into madness.

'Calm yourself, my boy, calm yourself. I am here as a friend, an ally of your father and mother. I can help you.'

Jack still hesitated, trembling.

'You *have* to trust me;' the man continued, 'there is no one else left. And I am afraid there is not much time. Your cousin acted bravely just now but extremely foolishly as well. She created a Pathway to... to... I don't know where. But the Pathway has closed behind her. See?' It was true. The white light had faded completely now. 'I may be able to re-open the Pathway, if we hurry.' He was already making his way to the staircase, passing Jack and taking his hand. He was wearing a long, black cloak, which swirled around him as he moved. 'Follow me and stay very close.'

'What pathway?' asked Jack. 'Who are you and how

do you know what happened here just now?'

The man was halfway up the stairs at the corner landing, dragging Jack along behind him. Their feet crunched on the pieces of the broken vase which Jack had knocked over earlier.

'I am Cleve Harrow. I know many things. Things of which you have no idea, not yet anyway. The Pathway is one of those things.

They had now reached the upper landing. The door to Helen's room was directly in front of them. It was still open.

Without hesitating, Cleve Harrow stepped down the hall and straight into the room. Jack hurried along behind him and heard him utter the words; 'Kron, appear to me'.

No sooner had he spoken than there was a whirring, fluttering sound. With a flash of blue light, Helen's Kron shot into the air from the drawer in the corner of the room, and flew straight into Harrow's outstretched hand. He held it up, balancing it on the tips of his broad fingers. It continued to glow with blue fire. Looking up at it from below, Jack thought that it looked like one of those colourful, round candles which lit up from the inside when the wick had burnt down far enough, so that all the colours showed up. However, this was much brighter, and far more beautiful. And unlike any candle that Jack had ever seen, the colours in the Kron changed. From blue it was now changing to pure bright white. 'It was orange for Helen,' he whispered, as if this piece of information were important for Cleve Harrow to know.

'And it should still be so. If it had kept the colour that she chose, orange, then there would still have been some of her power within it. I may have been able to use it to reverse her last actions downstairs. It might have re-opened the pathway through which she disappeared. But I am afraid that Helen is already truly out of our reach.'

'We can't get to her at all?' Jack asked, noticing a quiver in his voice.

'Let us hope that there are other ways to find her later.' Harrow replied. 'In any case, you must leave that to me.'

'Excuse me for appearing a bit thick,' said Jack. 'But what *is* the Kron?'

Harrow thought for a moment. He held the Kron aloft once more for Jack to see.

'A Kron is mostly used to Sidestep, to escape danger. The Select can do that, of course. Some can also use it for different magical purposes of their own – *if* the power of magic lies within them. Like many other tools or instruments, its power depends upon the skills of the person using it.'

'Where did the Kron come from?' Jack asked.

'Centuries ago,' Harrow continued, still cradling the globe in his fingers, 'this was fashioned by a wise man of great power and learning. A Mage'.

'I've heard of them' said Jack, pleased that he at last understood *something* that was being said to him. 'It's another name for a sort of magician.'

'Magician is a crude term for such learning and skill. Nowadays, in the minds of far too many people that word has come to mean one who creates tricks with playing cards, top hats and rabbits. An entertainer, a clown, a buffoon. But as that is the word you know then yes, a Mage *is* a kind of a magician.' He paused for a moment and Jack thought he seemed to grow taller. A grim smile curled on his lips. Harrow lowered his voice and looked deep into Jack's eyes. 'I prefer the term *wizard*.'

He now began to speak even more seriously than before. 'Imagine a *true* wizard, my boy. One who's knowledge of ancient lore and understanding of the world is immense. You will have heard of Merlin, no doubt?' Jack nodded and Harrow went on. 'He was a true wizard – a Mage,' Harrow continued sadly. 'And Merlin was one of the last great ones'.

'And are you a magici – sorry, a Mage?'

At this, Cleve Harrow did something as unusual, as unexpected, as anything else that had happened that evening: he laughed. His eyes crinkled up into gleeful little wrinkled slits and his mouth opened wide.

'No!' he roared. 'Not I. Although it is no wonder that you make such a suggestion after all that you have been through tonight.' His laughter faded and he became serious again – although Jack thought he could still see some remains of the bright twinkling in his eyes.

'I am not a Mage, Jack. Nor am I a Wizard. I am not even an ordinary 'magician' with a skill for card tricks. I studied to be a wizard, many years ago, but discovered that I do not have those powers. However, I have worked with several highly respected wizards and I continue to serve them in their struggles against the Rish. They taught me how to use the Kron, to travel the Pathways and certain other useful skills. My masters sit on the Council of the Wise in the Great Hall of Beltheron. In a way I am their agent. A spy, perhaps, in your words.'

'A spy?'

'I attempt to discover information about the Rish, their whereabouts and actions. I also spread rumour and lies to confound and confuse them whenever I can.'

'You've succeeded in confusing me tonight,' said Jack. 'I heard Uncle Matt and that tall man Parrynoon talking about the Rish; what are they?'

'The tall man's name is *Parenon* and he and your Uncle were talking of a very great evil. The Rish are servants of Gretton Tur, the Wild Lord of Atros, and they help him in his attempt to wreak havoc and misery on the three worlds:

their own world of Atros; in Beltheron, where Parenon and I live; and also here, on your own Earth. It is he, the evil Lord of Atros that we all fight against.'

Jack listened carefully. Earlier that night his uncle Matt had started to talk about other worlds, just before those Rish creatures had arrived at the house. His imagination struggled to come to terms with all this new information. Suddenly he yawned and shook his head briefly from side to side. Cleve Harrow's eyes narrowed with something like concern and pity. He put out a hand to pat Jack on the shoulder.

'You are weary, Jack. No wonder. You have learned much that is new and frightening to you and you are filled with worry for your parents and the others. There are those around who will help you though all this, my boy, myself not least among them. You must rest now. Try not to worry *too* much about Helen. We will begin our search for her tomorrow. In any case she may already have found safety.'

He looked around the room briefly.

'Nothing more will happen here tonight. The Rish have already taken great risks to show themselves here in your world, and to have acted with such abandon and fury. They will dare to do no more for a while. You are safe to relax and get some sleep. And in any event, I will be here to guard you.'

Tired as he was, Jack thought he had never been further from sleep in his life, but when Cleve Harrow showed him to his room, and he laid his head back on the pillows, he felt all his remaining energy drain from him. His eyes closed and within minutes he was breathing deeply, mouth open, his arms and legs twitching slightly as the tension left him.

Cleve Harrow sat by the bedside. He stared out of the window and then back at the sleeping boy, deep in thought for long periods of time, far into the night.

5
Travelling the Pathway

Jack awoke to the aroma of strong coffee and eggs and bacon. Bright sunlight streamed through the opened curtains and he could hear birds singing their greeting to the new day. All the memories of the previous night came flooding back to him in a rush: his missing parents, Parenon, Helen, Aunty Jenn and Uncle Matt's strange, garbled stories about his past, the violence in the house and everyone's unexplained disappearance.

Cleve Harrow stood in the entrance to the doorway, a large mug of steaming coffee in his hand.

'Good morning to you, Jack. It is now time you were up and about. Drink this while you get ready – then come straight downstairs. There is a good breakfast waiting for you. We must both eat heartily and well, for it is uncertain when we shall have the chance to do so again.'

He left Jack to change into fresh clothes. He opened his case, and saw the clothes lying there which his mother had helped him to pack only twenty four hours ago. He felt a huge emotion stirring up in his chest again. Instead of the threat of tears though, this time Jack felt a new determination, and anger.

'I'm going to find out what has happened,' he said firmly to himself. 'And I'm going to find Mum and Dad and everyone else. I'm going to help them. I don't know how, but I'm going to do whatever I can.' He quickly got ready; he put on jeans and his favourite trainers, with a sweatshirt. He hurried downstairs after Harrow, but his own brave words didn't really convince him, deep down inside.

When he walked into the kitchen, he saw straight away that Harrow had cleared away much of the debris and signs of the violent struggle of the night before. The tables and chairs had been righted, broken crockery had been swept away, and a number of boards were propped up against the smashed doorway. Sitting on the table were big platefuls of the eggs and bacon Jack had been able to smell, and a large pitcher of milk.

'There you are my boy. Sit, sit. Eat your fill.'

Gratefully, Jack hurried to a chair and started to do just that; he wolfed down the food in rapid forkfuls. He hadn't realised that he was so hungry. Harrow joined him at the table and began his own meal, though at a much more reasonable speed. Looking across the table at Jack, he smiled with affection.

When they had more or less finished their breakfast, Cleve Harrow began to speak.

'Now Jack, we must be getting down to business. We have a long journey ahead of us, but you still have much to learn. First of all, I must know how much you discovered last night. Please inform me of what you were told by Parenon and the others.'

'I don't really know where to begin Mr Harrow, Sir. They seemed to tell me an awful lot, but not much of anything that made sense. Not to me anyway.'

'Take your time Jack. And you need not call me *Mr* Harrow. Just plain Harrow will do if you are addressing me, or *the* Cleve, if you are talking about me to someone else. For Cleve is my title, do you see? It is *what* I am, not *who* I am.'

Jack did not see at all, but he nodded anyway.

'So,' continued the confusing Cleve, 'before we start out on our journey, may I suggest you now tell me everything you know about the other two worlds?'

Jack told him, as best he could, about all he had discovered the previous night; about the Rish, his special powers, and being the twenty-third generation of…of…of something or other. When he had finished, Harrow nodded and sat back in his chair. He poured another cup of steaming coffee for himself and began to speak.

'That is a great deal of information for one so young to have to understand. Let me set things out plainly for you.' He sipped at his coffee before continuing.

'Many years ago, long before you or your parents were born, a young boy lived in a small village in the land of Beltheron. Beltheron was a beautiful land; a world of peace and harmony. It was a place of great learning.' A faraway look came into the Cleve's eyes. A brief smile appeared on his lips, but it was obvious to Jack that the man was filled with sadness. Cleve Harrow shook his head and spoke again. 'Anyway, this boy was called Gretton Tur…'

'The same Gretton Tur you talked about last night, the one you called the, the *Wild Lord* or something?'

'Yes, the very same. But at the time I am now speaking about he was merely a young apprentice to a Mage. Gretton Tur was… he was…'

Cleve Harrow struggled to find the right words. Once more an expression of deep sorrow worked across his face. Jack wanted to ask more questions, but felt it would be best to let the Cleve continue when he was ready. So he waited and waited, it seemed like whole minutes on end, before his companion shook himself from his private thoughts and carried on with his tale.

'Gretton Tur was a wonderful student, quick and apt

with the old lessons. However, he became dissatisfied with his studies. He saw that he had abilities which could lead to great power. Tur began to look down on all the other apprentices he worked with. He saw himself as one who is far superior to everyone else, a King on a throne, or a great Lord in a palace. Gretton Tur coveted such things. His desire and hunger for power began to twist him up inside. Where there had once been a fine and promising young scholar, there now appeared a sneaking, secretive, malicious man. He trusted no one, and in turn, he himself became untrustworthy.'

Harrow paused, sipping at his coffee once more before continuing. 'He started to use the magical skills he was learning for strange and unknown purposes. Stories began to be told of how Gretton Tur had been seen alone in the fields at midnight, raising his arms to the sky and summoning lightning bolts from the clouds. Then things started to go wrong in Beltheron. Where once the land had been rich and fertile, now the dry barren soil would yield nothing, season after season. The happiness and friendship which had once been everywhere now turned to envy and hatred amongst neighbours - and even within families. Terrible violence erupted suddenly out of petty squabbles, and in the evening, mothers called in their children from the games they played in the streets, locking their doors behind them and pulling down the shutters. Before too long there were whisperings about the weird young apprentice who kept so much to himself and practised his magic secretly, late into the night. It was noticed that his nocturnal journeys into the fields coincided with the flooding of those same fields the following day, and that should anyone displease him in any way, a dreadful misadventure would befall that person before the sun set.

'So, in time, most people turned against Gretton Tur.

But some there were who followed him; they believed him to be a great Mage and a powerful leader; one who would bring them success and riches. Others travelled from neighbouring villages and towns with tales of his abilities ringing in their ears. They wished to join him. Tur gathered these people around him greedily and his power grew with their support. He and his surly, violent crew moved from the village, where by now there was scarcely anyone outside his own band who would speak to him, or even look him directly in the eye. They set up a low group of squalid looking dwellings at the edge of the forest, half a mile from the village, and from there they began their raids.'

Jack could tell that the story was painful for Harrow to relate. He had such a dreadful look of past suffering on his face as he continued in a desperate growl; 'Gretton Tur and I studied together under the tutelage of the same Master.'

'You studied with him? At the same time?' came Jack's disbelieving voice; 'but you said it was years and years ago.'

'Indeed it was, and, yes my boy, before you ask, I *am* old, very, *very* old by your reckoning. But I must finish my story! You must know all.

'When Tur's violence and hatred reached such heights that he could no longer be allowed to continue, he turned against our Master. There was a terrible battle of wills. The Master was utterly destroyed, but in his final breath he invoked a curse which banished Tur down the ancient Pathways to the renegade world of Atros. There he was to remain, imprisoned with no way back. However, during his long exile he spread evil throughout his new world, just as he had begun to do on Beltheron with his rag-tag band of followers. He sat in power in Atros, in the dark city of Gendrell, on a throne of his own creation. He summoned the Rish to serve him, dreadful creatures brought to life out of his own nightmares. He thought only of ways to revenge himself upon the land which had turned from him and sent him into exile.' Exhausted by his memories, Cleve Harrow slumped back in his chair. He looked as if he had aged by many years while he had been speaking, Jack thought, and for the first time he believed that Harrow really *was* an old man.

There was silence between them for a few moments, and then Jack dared to ask the question that had been on his mind for some time.

'What has all this got to do with *me*?'

Harrow roused himself again and looked directly into Jack's eyes. When he spoke it was with a renewed vigour. 'Now we come to the real business,' he said. 'You and Helen are both members of an ancient family. This family is called the *Select* of Beltheron. The Select are among the most important people in the land. They are blessed with many gifts and powers, as you are beginning to learn. Powers that people here on earth would call magic. The Select use these powers, this *magic*, in their fight against Gretton Tur. You, Jack, are about to enter that battle. Helen, of course, has had more time to get used to this. She has known from an early age what it means to be a Select. And not just *a* Select, but *twenty-third generation* Select! The ones who are spoken of in legend! Although your cousin Helen has known all of this since she was very young, your parents, for reasons of their own, chose not to tell you of your true history.'

Jack nodded, 'yes, my aunt and uncle started to tell me that last night.'

'Well, now that has to change.' The Cleve said. 'There is a special place for you in the battle I speak of. Many believe that you and Helen are destined to fulfil an ancient legend. There is an age old prophesy which says that somehow you and Helen can help to bring about the Wild Lord's final destruction. That is why you were both taken from Beltheron by your parents when you were born. It is why you were brought here, to Earth, so that you could both be hidden away safely from Tur and the Rish whilst your knowledge and powers grew. Then, when you were both ready, you could return and take your place in the struggle.'

'But if it was so important for Helen and I to join in the battle, and if we were hidden away here on Earth to get ready for it, then why did my parents not try to prepare me?' interrupted Jack.

'They grew fearful for you.' Harrow answered. 'Once on Earth, they thought that you would have a better, safer life if they turned their backs on Beltheron and the dangers of Atros altogether. They chose not to continue with the struggle.' Here Cleve Harrow paused and looked away for a moment, towards the corner of the room. His eyebrows bunched up as he scowled, deep in thought. 'Because,' he continued slowly, 'when you and Helen were still very young, the Pathways were opened up again by Gretton Tur. For the first time he himself discovered the ability to travel between worlds, and he sent out the Rish to begin their mad rampage of destruction.'

'How?' asked Jack. 'Weren't the Pathways safe? I thought you said that Gretton Tur had no power left?'

'Yes for many years they *were* safe, Jack. Their use was protected by strong magic, and we felt that they were closed forever, to all but the few Select who swore a solemn oath never to reveal their secrets, or allow others to travel through the Pathways with them. Parenon and I were only allowed to travel the Pathways to Earth a few days ago so that we could help to protect you and your family. But it appears that a traitor is working among us on Beltheron. I can think of no other way that Tur could have found a way to open the Pathways and use them for himself. Someone must have taken that knowledge to him. For over ten years now he has sent his armies and agents out into Beltheron. They raid farms and villages; they destroy buildings in gouts of fire. We have fought hard all this time. We have managed to contain the damage and the violence that they cause. But the powers of the Council of the Wise grow weak. The prophecy is coming true; Gretton Tur's power is on the rise and the Council needs the children of the twenty-third generation to return. Only then will the Council become strong again. Only then will the full meaning of the prophesy become clear. We need *you*, Jack. You and Helen'.

Harrow gazed at Jack for several moments before bringing his hands down heavily on the table with a loud thump. 'I am afraid I have talked too long, now we must be about our business'

Cleve Harrow rose from his place and walked over to a corner of the room. The long package that he had been carrying on the train was lying on the floor. Jack now realised that the package probably didn't contain either fishing rods or golf clubs, as he had originally guessed yesterday. But what *was* inside, he wondered?

'Clear some room for me on the table, my boy' ordered Harrow as he carried the package towards it. Jack quickly moved the remaining breakfast things and placed them in the kitchen sink. He hurried back to the broken table, his curiosity growing all the time.

As he looked closer he could see that the bag was made of some kind of tough looking, dark leather, almost black. Not quite black though, for all over it were scrawled strange words which were darker still, and seemed to be burnt into the heavy fabric. The words were in a language that Jack could not recognise, and even some of the letters themselves were unfamiliar. All along one side of the bag there were thin cords and buckles. Harrow was now busily unfastening them.

'Lend a hand there Jack' he said, nodding to the opposite end of the long bag to where he had started.

'Ok'.

Jack moved forwards uncertainly. Some of the knots looked very tight and complicated. There were so many of them running up and down the bag that he wondered if the Cleve had ever had to open it in a hurry. And if he did, how could he possibly manage it?

Not wanting to look a fool by getting the dense clumps of thin cord even more tangled, he hesitated. His fingers hovered centimetres above the first knot, wondering exactly where to start. Then as he was looking down at the cords, concentrating on them, a weird feeling ran quickly down his arms, making his fingers tingle. Before he knew what he was doing, he had unfastened the first set of cords. His fingers moved swiftly onwards, the knots almost disappearing beneath them. With a gasp of surprise, and then delight, he realised that as soon as his fingers touched the cords they began to *untie themselves,* snaking and unwinding rapidly, before settling down into little neatly coiled piles on either side of the bag. Cleve Harrow heard him chuckle at this amazing new discovery, and turned to him: 'Just one of your gifts, my young friend. You will discover many more in the coming days. There! You have already untied the final knot.'

Jack looked down. The bag lay open on the table and inside he saw a long, slender staff, carved with figures of men, women, and fabulous creatures. The staff was made of bright and shining solid gold.

'This is the Golden Staff of Beltheron.' Harrow spoke with tremendous reverence in his voice. 'The old magic is rich and powerful within it. This staff holds the secret of the Pathways of which I told you. It allows those whom the Select have chosen to travel the Pathways. Somehow, Gretton Tur has discovered the secret of its power. I believe that he has used the information passed on to him by his spy and, with that knowledge, he has fashioned his own staff, or some similar instrument, so that his Rish can travel through the worlds and wreak vengeance upon us all.'

Harrow lifted the Staff solemnly in his hands; 'Now Jack, take the end of the Staff, here.' He gestured towards the carving of a small figure near the bottom of the staff. Jack did as he was told and took hold. He looked closer at the carving and with a sharp intake of breath, said; 'Harrow! It looks like me!'

'Yes Jack. It is part of the prophesy. It was fashioned in your likeness, many years before you were even born. Look higher, just above your fingers; there you will see your cousin.'

Jack looked to where Harrow had indicated. There was another carving. Yes! It did look *just* like Helen, Jack thought. In fact, he considered Helen's image to be a much better likeness of her than his own carving was of him. He thought he looked a little bit...timid, the way his carved self peered out of the bright gold. He and Helen must be tremendously important he realised, to have been carved onto something as precious as this beautiful object.

Harrow began mumbling strange words. 'Velocior mediatus. Impregor volens!' His voice rose until he was shouting: 'Volens velocior! Velocior MEDIATUS!'

Nothing happened for a moment, and then; BANG! Jack thought that his ears must have exploded, the sound was so huge. It blocked out all other sensations for a moment. He could not see, hear or speak. Then there was a violent lurch and the ground tipped away from underneath his already shaking feet. Something grabbed the collar of his shirt and he was hauled upwards, almost losing his grip on the golden staff.

'Harrow, what's happening?'

'Keep hold Jack! We are about to travel the Pathway to Beltheron!'

Jack held on as tightly as he could. His vision suddenly cleared. He was in the middle of a spinning column of brilliant white light. Dizzy from turning and totally blinded by the dazzling flashes all around him, he and the Cleve screamed upwards. Jack thought for an instant about a dream he often had where he seemed to be falling, sucked down quickly so that his insides heaved. This was the same, but instead of plunging down he was being pulled up; and instead of the feeling going on for a couple of seconds, as it did in his dream, this went on and on. Already it felt as if whole minutes had passed. His arms and shoulders ached from hanging on to the staff, and his lungs felt bruised as he tried to catch his breath in the icy wind whipping past his face. Still they hurtled on and on. Up, up through the Pathway to Beltheron.

6
The Hunt of the Rish

Helen got to her feet carefully and looked around. She was standing on uneven ground amongst a group of rocks and patches of thin, dull green grass. About a mile away the ground rose up to form a range of hills, with high craggy mountains beyond. She was still wearing her pyjamas, dressing gown and slippers. 'Stupid,' she thought; 'why didn't I think to change?' She shivered. It was cold but a pale sun had just appeared over the horizon. Morning. Where had the liquid in the vial taken her? She looked down and saw that she still held the torn strip of pale blue cloth from Parenon's cloak. If the vial had worked properly, then Parenon must be somewhere nearby. While she gazed down at the fabric in her fingers, she caught sight of the rock at her feet. There lay the smashed vial, the last few drops of liquid spreading out across the ground. Helen closed her eyes for a moment in frustration. Without the liquid in the vial she didn't know how she was going to get back from… from wherever she was. She looked down at the ground again. Where she was standing the rock had been scorched black. She realised that she could feel the heat coming up from the ground through her slippers. 'I must have done that when I landed,' she said to herself. 'And there are some more scorch marks over there!'

In fact, as she inspected the rocks and grass nearby she discovered eight similarly burnt places. Reaching down to each one of these in turn, she found that they too were still warm under her fingers. 'That means they can't have landed very long ago,' she reasoned. 'If one of the marks was made by Parenon, then there are seven others with him.' Hopefully, her mother and father accounted for *two*, which still left another five. She straightened up from the last scorched mark and stood, thinking.

Five Rish. Five of those horrible creatures created out of Gretton Tur's own nightmares. Those horrible beings that she had heard so much about from her parents while she had been growing up, but had never seen until last night. She shuddered at the image of that long arm, snaking its way through the broken window, before it had been beaten back by Parenon's sword. For the first time, real fear gripped her. Until now she had been carried away with excitement. Poor Jack still hadn't understood what was going on, so it had been up to her to try to save them both. Everything had happened so quickly that she had had to take charge; making immediate decisions with barely any time to think. Now she was alone, with silence and stillness all around her, and her fear grew.

Where was she?

She thought back over her actions. By using the vial of liquid she had activated a Pathway to follow Parenon and – she hoped – her parents. But if the *Rish* had been in control, if *they* had won the fight in the kitchen – and she was now certain that even Parenon could not have defeated *five* creatures such as that – then they would have opened up a Pathway back to their own land. And if that was the case, then she had followed them right into the kingdom of their leader, the evil Gretton Tur the Wild! With a cold feeling of dread, Helen realised that she was standing – all alone – on the renegade world of Atros.

As she stood there wondering what to do next she

heard a sound behind her. Her heart leapt and she spun around, terrified of what might be there. It was only a lizard, about twelve centimetres long, which was scuttling over the stony ground. She must have disturbed it, she thought. The lizard had a long spiked tail which it flicked wickedly from side to side. It was bright orange and red, and it had too many legs to count. The lizard turned to Helen, grinning widely to show pointed, grey teeth, before sticking its rough tongue out at her and hurrying off. Helen shuddered. She made a face at its retreating tail. 'Yuk, disgusting thing.' Then there was another sound, as more lizards ran out of their hiding places. Behind her she heard a flutter in the air as a large bird took off from a tall clump of grass about ten metres away.

'That isn't *me* disturbing them,' she realised; 'it's someone else.'

Just as this thought crossed her mind the earth beneath her feet began to tremble, and a low rumble could be heard from the direction of the hills. Helen looked from side to side in rising panic, as the approaching sound grew louder. 'Hooves,' she thought, 'and lots of them.'

There was nowhere she could hide. Instinctively her hand went to her pocket. She needed the Kron, she would have to Sidestep, and quickly. But the Kron was not there. Of course! She had left it behind. 'Stupid, stupid, stupid!' she told herself. There was nothing for it. To stand there was to have no hope, to be caught without a doubt. Helen turned away from the direction of the clattering hooves and scanned the land ahead of her for any signs of possible shelter. There were none to be seen. She could now hear the additional sound of loud, whinnying cries. The same whinny that she had heard outside the kitchen windows at home the night before. 'Holva,' Helen thought. She began to run. She ran faster than she had ever thought she could, tripping in her bedroom slippers and stumbling in her panic over the uneven, rough ground.

As Helen ran she dared a quick look behind her. About a hundred metres away a group of horse-like creatures was galloping towards her, gaining all the time. It had only been a glance of a couple of seconds, but it was enough for Helen. These 'horses' were huge – almost twice the size of an ordinary horse back on earth. She knew these were Holva, the creatures that the Rish rode when they hunted. Instead of hair, manes and tails the Holva were covered in a grey, scaly skin, like a reptile. Their heads were like horse skulls, and instead of bits and bridles to control them, cruel spikes had been driven through their bony cheeks and attached to dark chains that their riders held. It was these riders that horrified Helen most, even more than the outlandish horse-creatures; for these were the Rish and she knew that they meant to kill her. She recognised their long, snake-like arms from the glimpse she got of the one which had tried to break through the window during the battle in the kitchen. However, Helen hadn't realised that the Rish had *four* arms each, instead of two. Her parents hadn't told her that. The Rish's heads were long and oval – like an egg that had somehow been stretched out of shape – with blank, grey faces whose only features were dark slits for eyes, ears and nostrils. The Rish heads ended in a beak for a mouth like a bird's, but when *these* mouths opened, they showed row upon row of jagged black teeth.

Helen knew that she could not escape. The long legs of the Holva were closing in too quickly. But still she ran on. Fear drove her. She heard a triumphant wailing scream from one of them. They must have seen her and in that moment she thought she would be sick. Terror heaved up into her throat but she swallowed it down, still plunging and twisting through the rocks in her desperate flight. The ridiculously out-of-place dressing gown flapped wildly about her legs and she lost one of her slippers. The noise became unbearably loud and close, snorting, clattering, wailing. She turned again; back to face her pursuers, lifting her arm to protect herself from the blow that she knew must come at any moment. She took another final step back just as the bone-like heads of the horse-creatures and the long Rish arms filled her world... and then she stumbled. Falling backwards now, the ground disappeared under her feet, and with both arms flailing madly to try to keep her balance, she tumbled and skidded down a steep embankment.

Three or four of the horse-creatures reared at the top of the slope. They pulled back, snickering and whinnying in fear and anger, their riders fighting for control.

However, the other two Holva and their riders followed Helen down the hill without a pause. They skidded, their cloven hooves digging and churning in the pebbles and stones, missing Helen's crazily cartwheeling figure by centimetres. An arm almost grabbed one of her legs, and hot spittle splashed her cheek.

The next moment she felt the ground open underneath her. Screaming with what felt like her last ounce of breath, she tumbled into blackness. She fell for two or three seconds, spiralling through the air before landing with a heavy thud on the cold ground. Aching in every part of her body, she lay there, perfectly still. The noises from above seemed very distant now, as she felt herself fading away. 'Is this it then?' she thought, 'is this the end? You stupid girl Helen Day! Stupid, stupid, stupi...' then blackness closed around her.

Surprisingly though, as she lost consciousness, her last thought was not of despair, but one of hope. For slung across the saddle of one of the horses, among the riders at the top of the slope, she thought that just for an instant – just before she fell – she had glimpsed the flash of a pale, blue cloak.

Helen had no idea how long she had been unconscious. It must only have been for a minute or so. When she came to her senses the voices of the Rish could still be heard above her. The garbled noise they made was a horrible mixture of high pitched screams and low, guttural shouts that sounded like a barking cough. They were peering into the hole that Helen had fallen through. It appeared that they had not yet found a way down into the cavern where she was now lying, some five metres below. The rock floor was hard and smooth under her. Helen felt dizzy from the chase and her dreadful fall. She gingerly opened her eyes and waited for her vision to swim back into focus. The first thing that she saw was a patch of blue sky above the hole in the cavern roof. Suddenly, the silhouette of one of the Rish leant over the hole and looked in, its smooth, egg-shaped head turned to one side and then the other as it gazed down, trying to find her. It must have made her out at last in the dimness, for with a triumphant shriek it coiled a long arm through the hole. Grasped in its hand was a narrow, jagged spear. The Rish jabbed around with it angrily trying to get to Helen but the cavern was too deep by far; even with those long arms, the terrible creature couldn't get close.

'Even so;' thought Helen, 'I can't just lie here and wait for one of them to have the brilliant idea of jumping down, or for the ground to give way some more and have the whole lot of them just fall on top of me.' She tried to get to her feet but wobbled unsteadily. She winced as a sharp pain shot up her side. She tried again. This time she managed it, even though every single part of her body ached. Her head throbbed and Helen found that her left foot was particularly painful as she placed her weight on it. As soon as she began to move, the noise above her erupted into a choking, howling babble of rage. The Rish that had tried to jab her with the spear now flung it down the hole in frustration at her. It clattered harmlessly onto the floor next to her, to even more cries of anger from above.

Helen bent and picked it up. 'Thanks Guys! Now at least I'm armed!' However she didn't feel as brave as her words made out. In truth, she was still terrified. In spite of the pain in her foot she hobbled quickly out of the patch of light and – she hoped – out of their sight. Her shoulder struck the wall in the darkness. 'What if this isn't a cavern,' she thought; 'what if it's just some sort of pit with no way out or' – a new idea struck a fresh chill into her heart – 'or even a *trap*.'

No. She would *not* believe that. With the spear clenched tight in one fist, and her other hand in front of her, feeling carefully every inch of the way, Helen moved along the wall away from the shaft of sunlight and those terrifying cries.

Although she had twisted her left foot badly, Helen found to her relief that she could limp along on it, and she didn't think that anything was broken.

The rock wall of the cavern was smooth and cold under her fingers. It curved slowly around a corner, and following it, she soon passed out of sight of the hole. For a moment, all was blackness again. By now though, her eyes had begun to adjust to the cavern and she thought she saw more light way, way ahead of her. At first it was just a pale smear in the distance, but as she focused her eyes on it, colours and shapes started to appear. She saw morning sunlight dappling a patch of rock. A way out!

As her hopes began to rise there was a crash behind her, two thudding sounds and the triumphant yells of the Rish. 'They're through!' thought Helen and instantly hurried forwards. She could not run fast because of the pain in her foot, and even though her instincts fought against her rushing madly over uneven rocks in the dark, a deeper terror of what was behind her drove her quickly onwards. She groped ahead, waving the spear in one hand to check her way was clear. Her feet scraped and stumbled along. Her pursuers must surely have heard her! The Rish however, were making so much racket amongst themselves that they obviously hadn't. Even so she tried to make less noise as she fled towards the distant light. Once more the thought of the pale blue cloak spurred her on. Parenon! She was certain that she had seen him slumped across one of the nightmare-horse's backs. She *must* get to him. She *must* find Parenon.

The light ahead was getting closer now; there were only a hundred metres or so left to go. Helen could see the opening clearly. It was not very large, but just big enough for her to crawl through. (She hoped.) Big enough for her; but not, perhaps, for her large pursuers. Onwards she ran. Onwards. With the throbbing pain in her head, and the agony of her twisted foot. Onwards. Not far now.

The sounds behind her started to get louder. The voices had stopped but she could hear the regular beat of footsteps hurrying in her direction. Somehow in the darkness the Rish had found her trail. She looked back. A flickering light appeared around the corner. They had a torch! Two Rish hurled themselves up the cavern path towards her. The one in front held the blazing torch high over his head, and in the red and orange glow Helen could see the smooth, slitted face. The beak-mouth opened wide in the excitement of the chase, and he was slavering – the spittle reflecting in the torch light – as if he were hungry. To stay and fight – even with the spear – would be useless. She turned and ran on. Fifty metres to go. Ignoring the pain Helen sped towards the opening. She had been right though; the hole wasn't very large. It was a narrow, horizontal crevice near the floor of the cavern. The roof sloped sharply down to meet it, so much that she already had to crouch down as she ran. With only a few paces to go, she dropped to her hands and knees, with her head and shoulders scraping the roof. Finally she had to wriggle on her stomach to reach the opening.

The footsteps behind were very close now as she squeezed the top of her body through the narrow gap. She was half way through! She had made it! But just as bright sunlight hit her face, a cold hand grabbed her ankle. She screamed and struggled desperately to try to free herself. The Rish tried to pull her back through the opening, back into the cavern. It was twisting her leg around and sharp bolts of agony shot up through her already damaged foot and into the small of her back. In rising panic she kicked out with the last of her strength, and tried to force the spear back through the hole to stab her attackers. Still the Rish held on and pulled. She could hear it growling and snarling. The rock at the top of the crevice was cutting into her ribs as she was forced back inside. Helen felt as if her leg must surely be jerked out of its socket; the pain was so terrible that she felt she might lose consciousness again. She shook her head to clear it and pulled forwards once more. It was no good; the Rish was too strong. It was still dragging her backwards...

7
Arrival in Beltheron

The small circular room was cluttered with boxes and books. An old table in the middle had maps and other documents spread out over it. There were ancient charts hanging at odd angles on the walls covered with strange lettering, roughly drawn pictures and tiny diagrams. It was obviously a study of some kind. The room was at the very top of a tall, crumbling tower. It was lit only by a number of lamps and candles; there were no windows. The study could only be reached through a door leading to a narrow stone staircase which wound up around the *outside* of the building. There was no handrail to hold onto, and the steps were so uneven and broken with age and long use, that few people attempted the climb. This meant that the occupant of the study was usually left alone to her work. This suited her just fine. She did not need company. She was far too busy and other people only got in her way; wasted her time. At the moment she was kneeling on the floor, huddled over a huge black book with yellowing pages. The book was so large, and looked so heavy, that it was much easier for the woman to get down on all fours to read it, than it was for her to try to lift it up onto the table. Her fingers sped across the page as she murmured the words under her breath.

The woman was dressed in a long robe of pure white. The first thing that could be seen of her as she crouched down over the book on the floor was her hair; it too was pure, pure white just like her cloak, and anyone coming across her like this would probably think that she was old.

At that moment however, with a happy cry of victory, she leapt to her feet, and throwing her arms in the air with delight, tossed back her head and laughed. No one seeing her *now* could think that she was old, for in spite of her white hair it was obvious that the woman was very young, hardly twenty years old. Young she was, and extremely beautiful. She continued to laugh, and the joy lit up her whole face. Some people laugh, or smile with only their mouths, while their eyes remain dead and dark, but hers twinkled with pleasure and mischief. She skipped around the small room to the table in the middle, still chuckling, and now talking to herself.

'I knew it was in there; I knew I'd seen it before.'

The young woman began rummaging among the charts and papers on the tabletop. After a moment she gave another little whoop of joy and discovery. 'Here it is!'

She picked up a piece of paper and carried it back to the book on the floor. The paper had a small diagram faintly scribbled on it in red ink. She began comparing it with a picture in the book, humming to herself every now and then in satisfaction.

The woman had just begun to make some notes of her own about her find, when the air began to vibrate. There was a low humming, followed by a rushing, whistling sound in her ears and then, with a sudden flash, a white column of light appeared in the centre of the room. The light and the humming sound both faded and there stood Cleve Harrow and Jack Anders.

Jack was still gripping tightly onto the golden staff with both hands and his eyes were clamped shut. 'It's alright now, my boy,' chuckled Harrow; 'you can open them. Here we are. Welcome to Beltheron, or to be more accurate, my study, in the heart of Beltheron's capital city.' Jack did as he was told and slowly peeped through one eye. The first thing he saw was the beautiful, white haired young woman, who was gazing back at him. She had a curious, questioning look in her eyes, but still kept a friendly smile on her lips.

'Orianna my dear,' continued Cleve Harrow; 'how lovely to see you. Jack, allow me to introduce my very best student. (Not to mention my favourite!) Orianna Melgardes. She has been absolutely invaluable to me recently in finding out more of the history of Atros, and of the activities of the Wild Lord.'

'Delighted to meet you, Jack. I have heard a great deal about you and your family. This is an honour indeed.' Orianna stretched her hand out towards him and he shook it, feeling his cheeks begin to burn bright red in embarrassment. He had never seen anyone so beautiful in his life.

'Hello' he managed to mumble in reply.

Orianna Melgardes chuckled and turned to Harrow. 'The poor lad is overwhelmed by his journey. Let him sit here quietly for a few minutes while I tell you of what I have just learned.'

'You are making progress?' Harrow replied.

'Oh yes!' Her eyes sparkled even more.

'Speak then my dear, and quickly.'

The two of them seemed to forget about Jack immediately as Orianna showed the Cleve the paper she had just been looking at. Jack caught a glimpse of the picture that had been drawn on it. It looked like the small bottle of liquid that Helen had used to open the pathway when she followed Parenon.

'This is what Vishan saw during his last raid on the Rish caverns.' Orianna said. 'We know that Tur has created his own staff somehow, in the style of the Golden Staff of Beltheron and that is how he has managed to make Pathways of his own. But look! They now have a vial as well! To make such a thing, someone *must* have given them one of the original ones created here on Beltheron!'

'Yes, yes I see.' Harrow murmured, looking closely at the drawing. 'And Vishan was quite sure?'

'You know how precise he is. He would not make a mistake. And when has his information ever let us down before?'

'Quite so my dear. Well, this at least proves that there *is* a spy in our midst – there is no other way they could have got their hands on a vial and known how to use it.'

'Not only that, but remember how the liquid in the vial works;' Orianna continued eagerly; 'you must have some other artefact, something that belongs to the person you wish to follow, before you can create a Pathway to them. It is a rare skill indeed, one that very few of the Select in history have possessed. It is only the Lady Helen who has been able to do it for generations. Very few people are even aware of the skill any more.'

Cleve Harrow nodded in agreement. 'Yes. Helen and her parents know of the power of the vials of course. There are the two of us, who have studied them, Ungolin also knows and maybe just a handful of others.'

The two of them were thoughtful for a few moments. Then Orianna spoke. 'If this vial is the way the Rish are travelling between worlds, then the traitor must be very close to us. It must be someone who knows where to find such things.'

Harrow nodded vigorously. 'Yes! We thought it could be anyone on the Council, or any guard or Mage who worked in the city, but this means our search is now much simpler.'

'And more worrying, Cleve,' Orianna added; 'because

it also means that the spy, the traitor, is probably a friend.'

Harrow's eyes clouded. He looked very severe for a moment. 'That is true. We will think on this further and talk again. But now there is most urgent business to be attended to. Forgive me Orianna my dear, but we must leave your discoveries for later.' He broke off and walked across the room in two strides to a small bookcase along one wall. From a high shelf he gently lifted down a glowing green globe, about the size of an orange. Turning towards Jack, Harrow held the object out to him.

'For you, Jack. It is high time that you had a Kron of your own.'

Jack stepped forwards slowly. 'Thank you Harrow. It's…it's beautiful. But I don't know how to use it.'

The Cleve and Orianna both smiled at him. 'Don't worry about that.' Orianna said. 'The Cleve here is an excellent teacher and I am sure he would consider it a great privilege to instruct you.'

'Yes, and I will do so very soon.' His hands reached out to clutch Jack's own. 'Keep the Kron most safely my boy, for it is an object of enormous value and could be vital for your safety in the times to come. Now, both of you follow me.'

Harrow walked towards the oak doorway and opened it. Jack put the Kron carefully into his pocket, making sure it was pushed right down to the bottom. The weight of the globe felt strangely reassuring.

Jack looked past Harrow and out through the door to see a deep blue sky with pale clouds whipping rapidly across it. A cool breeze blew through the door and onto Jack's face. 'This staircase is the only way down,' said Harrow as he led the way out of the room and onto a platform. As Jack looked past Harrow he realised that the Cleve was standing at the top of the narrow stone staircase that wound down the outside of the tower. He gulped as he realised that that was the way down.

'Stay close to the wall, Jack.' The Cleve said. 'As you can see there is no rail to hold onto and it is a long, long drop to the bottom.'

It was indeed a long way down. As he followed Harrow out of the door, with Orianna Melgardes close behind them, Jack looked out over the rooftops and towers at a great, sprawling city. He stopped in the doorway and gasped in amazement at what he saw spread out below him. He hadn't realised that the room he was standing in had been *so* high up. Orianna put a hand on his shoulder; 'incredible isn't it?' she whispered in his ear. 'Take a moment to enjoy your first view of the capital city of Beltheron.'

The city was immense. It stretched as far as the horizon in every direction he could see. Some of the other buildings and spires were even taller than the one he stood on. Huge birds, the shape of hawks and eagles, circled and swooped around them, and the tops of the very tallest towers were hidden in the clouds themselves. Many of these high buildings looked extremely old, with crumbling black brickwork, but there were also other, very different buildings, ones which shone with newness. They had smooth curving shapes of metal and concrete disappearing into the mists above him. His eyes dropped from these high towers to look down at the city itself. For a moment his vision blurred and he became dizzy, clutching at the doorframe to support himself. He felt Orianna's hand squeeze his shoulder a little more tightly.

At first all he was aware of was a patchwork of different shapes in hundreds of colours. Then, as his dizziness passed and his vision cleared, the shapes took on the appearance of buildings, fields and parks. There were cathedrals, streets full of houses, markets and long, low buildings that he guessed might be factories or maybe train stations.

'It's beautiful.' He whispered.

'It is indeed. Come, let us go down.'

Orianna still held onto his arm as they descended from the tower. Jack tried to keep as close to the wall as he could on the narrow steps. Even so, the open view over the rooftops without even a handrail for security, made his head swim with vertigo. Twice he almost stumbled on the old crumbling staircase, gasping each time as he imagined hurtling down to the streets below.

Down, down they went. Jack thought it would have been a good idea to count the steps, but now it was far too late to start. He imagined they had already come down more than three hundred. And still they were not nearly at the bottom. However, he could hear the sounds of busy city life rising from the streets. They were now on a level with many more buildings, and after his aching legs had carried him down about another one hundred and fifty steps they arrived at last on the ground.

Jack was exhausted. It had been slow progress because of the uneven stairs, and it had taken them over half an hour to climb down. (He wasn't looking forward to having to climb back up any time soon!) Cleve Harrow would not let them rest, however. He set off straight away, with Orianna following him, turning and gesturing for Jack to keep up.

The three figures walked through the busy, bustling streets. Some areas of the city were tightly packed with houses and people, so that they had to struggle, push and excuse themselves through the crowds. Brightly coloured flags flew from many of the buildings and had been stretched across some of the roads from poles and windows. The three of them reached an open park with wide avenues of trees and swan-covered lakes. There were more flags strung from the trees. Through the park they went and then back to more city streets. There was a market taking place and voices called out from every side. Strange and wonderful smells filled Jack's nostrils; spices, cooking meats, perfumes. His eyes were everywhere at once, and his head was full of questions. There were some people travelling on carts pulled by donkeys, cattle or small horses, while others rode bicycles. Nothing so very strange in this, but what made Jack stare in surprise was the fact that, as well as these, there were a few other citizens who whizzed past them on motorised vehicles; smooth, bright metallic looking things which floated several inches off the ground.

'How do they do that?' he breathed.

'Some use their magic powers in that way, mixed with a little science.' Harrow replied.

'But if you have that power here in Beltheron, why doesn't everyone do it; instead of using the carts and the bicycles?'

'Not everyone does have the power, Jack;' answered Orianna.

'But doesn't that cause arguments?' Jack went on. 'Don't the people without the power to create those machines get jealous?'

Orianna smiled. 'I suppose it could cause jealousy. But here on Beltheron it is understood and accepted that each person has his or her own gifts. Every one is valued here because each one of those gifts is considered to be important in its own way. They all have their place; a part in the fabric of our society. So if anyone is in real need or danger, then others will come to their aid without question.'

Jack thought about this. It sounded very simple. He wondered if things could ever be made to work like that on earth. He doubted it.

'Besides,' Orianna continued. 'There are many who merely *choose* not to use these things. For some people, the flying machines are a little bit like exciting toys; great fun, but not to be taken seriously. I myself have many powers, and yet I still prefer to use these to get around' She raised one leg slightly and waggled her foot. There was a hissing sound in the air nearby. Orianna looked up and smiled. 'Mmm. The flying machines can be useful sometimes though.' She pointed towards a woman in a smartly cut red velvet suit just as her vehicle, shaped a bit like an egg (but with fitted cushions and with handlebars sprouting from the front) shot up vertically into the air to avoid a particularly slow moving carthorse. The woman sped off over their heads towards a large modern looking building at the end of the street.

'That's terrific;' laughed Jack, 'at Christmas I think I'll ask Mum and….' He stopped. Pain flooded back into his mind. Mum and Dad. He was still no closer to finding out where they were, if they were safe from the Rish, or if they were even… Jack shuddered and dropped his head. Both Harrow and Orianna knew what he was thinking, and straightaway Harrow spoke in a bright, optimistic voice: 'we are almost there. Come my friends, to the Great Hall, where we are sure to find answers to our questions, and who knows what else besides.'

They continued through the city until a great grey building loomed above them. At the top of a broad set of steps leading up to the building, two stone pillars stood on either side of a huge wooden door. Jack thought that it looked like a palace, and guessed that the Great Hall must be somewhere inside. Harrow, Jack and Orianna climbed the steps until they were challenged by three guards standing to attention at the top. They were dressed in leather breeches and jackets, and each one held a long, curving sword. From their shoulders hung pale blue cloaks. 'Just like Parenon's cloak,' Jack thought to himself, and the memory of that heroic figure immediately gave his spirits a boost.

One of the guards had begun to grin as they approached him. 'Why, it's The Cleve! Welcome to you, sir, and to your companions.'

'Thank you, er, Cannish isn't it?'

The guard beamed even wider. 'Cannish it is sir. You know Gennel, my brother. He was your guide last summer when you made your journey into the Far Forest to collect herbs. And very kind of you to remember me sir, what with all the things that must be swimming around in your head. Matters of State, the fate and future of all Beltheron.... But excuse me sir for prattling on when you must have important business to attend to.' Cannish turned to his two companions. 'Felior! Drannon! Make haste, make haste! The Cleve here has work to do. Open the doors, the doors I say!'

The guards went quickly about their business and the doors swung open with a deep, creaking groan. The three walked through, Harrow turning back as he passed the guards, 'Many thanks to you Cannish, and do pass on my remembrances to Gennel.'

'That I will sir, that I will. Always a pleasure to see you, sir.'

The doors closed behind them with a deep boom. They were inside. More steps rose in front of them, leading to the Great Hall itself. A dim light shone down from narrow windows high, high above them, making long, slanting shadows on the floors and walls. There were more guards at either side of the wide stairs as they climbed, dressed in the same leather breeches and jackets as Cannish, Felior and Drannon, but instead of the blue cloaks, the ones worn by these men were deep crimson. Jack wondered if they were a different rank of soldier, and if being *inside* the palace meant that they were more important. In any case, their cold expressionless faces made him feel very ill at ease as he climbed.

At the top of the staircase they came to an immense picture of a violent battle. Jack thought that it was a painting at first, but when he looked closely he saw stitches, and an uneven surface, which in some places was built up with many, many layers of thread. It was a tapestry, Jack realised, and it covered the entire width of the broad staircase, hanging right down to the floor from where it was suspended from the very heights of the ceiling way above his head. His jaw dropped open at the sheer size of it.

'Wow!' Jack said in a whisper; 'there must be over a million stitches!'

'Seventeen million, four hundred and eighty three thousand, six hundred and ninety one.' Said Orianna. 'That is the official figure anyway. But don't take my word for it Jack; I haven't actually counted them myself.'

Jack turned back to the ornate picture of colourful threads. He craned his neck upwards to see more. At the centre of the tapestry, about three metres above his head, was the image of a warrior on horseback. He looked fierce and extremely strong; one hand held the reins of a rearing horse, its hooves pawing savagely at the air; in the other hand the warrior held a long bright sword. Jack noticed red stitching at the sword's tip, indicating blood, and looking further down the tapestry he saw a headless body about to be trampled underfoot by the horse. Its head was lying by a tree trunk on the other side of the path. Suddenly he gasped as the body in the picture moved! Its arm jerked sideways and Jack stepped back in alarm. Then he laughed at himself; of course it wasn't the *body* that was moving, only the picture! Cleve Harrow had moved towards it and lifted a panel of it to one side to create an opening for them all to walk through. The picture rippled as the fabric folded, and for a moment Jack watched as the severed head seemed to reconnect itself to the body of the slain man! Orianna was already stepping into the room beyond. Jack followed her and realised that the tapestry was not one massive piece of cloth, as he had thought at first. In fact there were several long panels hanging down like curtains and it was onto these panels that the tapestry had been sown. It had been done so skilfully that it was almost impossible to see where one panel ended and another began. Jack had helped to hang wallpaper at home last year when his bedroom had been redecorated and so he knew how difficult it was to line up the patterns. 'Wow!' he said again as he passed under the heavy folds of material.

'Follow behind me,' Orianna was saying, 'and watch your step. It is darker here and the floor is old and uneven.'

It was very dark. The panel of the tapestry swung closed behind them so that the only light in the passageway came from a couple of guttering torches on the walls. At the far end, Jack could just make out another doorway, and from behind it came the murmur of many voices.

'Where are we going Orianna?'

'Up ahead is the doorway to The Great Hall. You are going to meet the Council of the Wise.' She answered. 'They are expecting you. The return to Beltheron of one of the Select is a great event.'

This made Jack even more nervous. 'I wonder what it is they want with me?' he thought. 'I don't seem to have been much use to anyone so far.'

'Stay close to us and be careful of what you say from

now on.' Harrow warned him. 'Remember that the traitor could be in our midst in the next couple of minutes.'

One final guard stood directly in front of the door at the end of the passageway. This one, however, was not a man as the others had been. The figure was short, a couple of centimetres smaller than Jack himself, but it was as broad as it was tall. The head was like that of a dog, and sat between the creature's shoulders, with no neck at all. Three pairs of arms sprouted from the torso, all of them of different lengths and thickness. Two of the arms ended in human hands, two in paws and the final two – on the lowest limbs – had sharp pincers attached. Jack couldn't see any legs at first, but as they approached, the figure seemed to grow in front of him, rising up on two sturdy limbs that opened out like telescopes. The dog-like head lunged forward, and in a rasping, ugly voice it snarled; 'whaddyewanineere?'

Cleve Harrow answered in a strong, clear voice. 'Noble beast of the Lodden Mountains, we are here on urgent business to see Ungolin, the leader of the Council of the Wise. My companions are Orianna Melgardes, a dedicated and able scholar, and young Jack Anders, an honourable *twenty-third generation* of the Family of the Select. We are here to assist in the struggles against your enemy and ours: Gretton Tur the Wild.'

The creature made a strange movement and bent forwards 'It's *bowing* to us!' Jack realised. Then with even more amazement he thought; 'No! Not to us. It's bowing to *me*!'

'Ayamonoredinbeeinaservisstewyew.' The creature rasped. 'Pleezennertheeawl.' The beast stretched out one of its middle arms (the ones with the paws) and opened the door.

The room was a blaze of light, and filled with people.

More tapestries hung from the walls, covered in fabulous greens, blues and gold. In the centre of the Great Hall burned a tremendous fire. The smoke swirled away in a dark column through a hole in the middle of the ceiling. All faces turned to see them enter. There were many cries of delight and wonder as several people surged forwards to get a closer look. And in all the crowded mass, the first faces that Jack saw were those of Aunty Jenn and Uncle Matt.

8

Conversation by Firelight

Parenon was lurched back to his senses with a jolt of pain through his back. He was being thrown around, up and down, backwards and forwards. His first thought was that he was about to vomit. He risked opening his eyes. They were met with a blurred image of the rocky ground speeding past. A stink hit his nostrils. It was a foul stench that he recognised all too well; "Holva" he grunted. Ropes and tight cords were biting into the skin on his wrists. The fabric around his sleeves felt slick and wet. Even in his confused, delirious state he realised that it was his own blood that was soaking his garments.

He shook his head to try to clear it and received a vicious thump on his ear. Parenon felt a calloused hand push him back onto the rear of the saddle where he had been slung and tied. "Be Still!" The rasping shout was unmistakable. He risked a look around him. The huge Holva that was carrying him was spurred on by one of the vicious Rish soldiers, and the stench coming from him was even worse than that of the Holva itself. There were six or seven of them, and they were all galloping across a plain. Parenon looked ahead, in the direction they were going. The pain increased in his temples as he raised his head but in a few moments his vision began to clear. The ground fell away about two hundred metres in front of them and Parenon thought that he glimpsed a familiar figure on the horizon line. In his confused state it took him a couple of moments to realise who it was.

"Lady Yelenia!" he gasped, and a new determination suddenly rose up inside him. The Holva were hunting down the poor, defenceless girl, and he was the only one able to stop them.

They galloped on towards the dropping ground ahead and plunged down the slope. By now Helen had scrambled ahead down the slope. Parenon tried to keep his eyes on her and gasped as she disappeared from view. Where she had been standing only moments before there was now just a dark hole in the earth. For a moment he thought that she must have sidestepped, but realised with a shock that she had fallen through into a cavern below. The Holva were now slowing and the attention of the riders was taken up with shouting at each other and controlling their steeds. Parenon took his chance and twisted around. They had taken his sword, but not the knife tucked securely into his long leather boot. As the Holva swerved to a halt he used the momentum to reach down to grab the knife and, with one swift movement, sliced through the cord that held him to the saddle. He rolled off its back to land with a breath-crunching thump on the ground. A moment later, the Rish soldier who had been riding with him landed a few feet away. He turned on Parenon with a frightening snarl and his long arms reached towards him. There were daggers in the creature's hands and he slashed at Parenon's face. The soldier leapt backwards, spinning high in the air to alter his direction and throw the Rish off balance, and then lunged forwards with his own knife aimed at the Rish's left eyeball. It struck home, and with a bone chilling cry the injured Rish staggered to his knees, clutching at his face. Black blood gushed between its clawed hands. Parenon pushed his attack forwards and struck again with the knife. Desperation drove him on. He moved swiftly and smoothly, a highly trained soldier at the stretch of his powers. Even in the midst of the fight, as he delivered the final death blow to the monster he was aware of the rest of the Holva disappearing down the slope ahead of him, in pursuit of Helen.

The Holva that he had just jumped from was still a few metres away, whinnying and madly churning its heels in anger. Parenon stepped towards it without hesitation and grabbed hold of the chains around its neck. The creature was strong and pulled away from him, but Parenon knew that he had to master this steed, or he would never catch up with Helen's pursuers in time. He had a handful of seconds at the most before it would be too late to save her. He jerked down roughly on the chains and with a whinny of shock, the holva slowed its movements long enough for Parenon to jump onto its back. With his favourite cry of 'for Mage and Council!' instilled in him from month's of hard training on Beltheron (and hard drinking in the inns with his fellow soldiers) Parenon kicked his heels into the holva's sides. They were off at a sudden gallop.

The Rish up ahead of him were gaining on the dim figure of the child running ahead. He could only just make her out through the haze of dust raised by the holva's galloping hooves. He *had* to reach her in time, he just *had* to. Memories flooded into Parenon's mind of others he had let down long ago, others in his own family whom he had not been able to save. He thrust the painful thoughts aside and spurred the holva on even faster, leaning low over the creature's neck.

As he felt himself drawing nearer to his quarry something caught his eye on the ground ahead. At first he couldn't make out what it was. It looked like a bright flash of colour that looked quite out of place on the bare plain. As he drew closer he recognised it with a pang. Helen's slipper! Swinging low over one side of the saddle he scooped it up in his fingers as they sped past; he tucked it securely into his blue tunic. When he looked back towards the group of Rish and holva up ahead a strange thing happened. Helen had disappeared. The Rish were reining in the holva and calling to each other in their piercing screeches. Parenon's ears ached at the sound of it. He struggled to see past them, to work out where Helen had gone.

As he approached, he saw the hole in the ground. Two of the Rish had dismounted and were gazing down into the black hole below. Parenon leapt from the holva's back and threw himself behind a large clump of rocks. More of the Rish were now getting off their steeds and peering into the hole.

An argument was growing amongst the creatures as they tried to decide how best to proceed. It was now clear to Parenon exactly what had happened, and he prayed fervently that Helen had not been too badly hurt by the fall into the cavern below. He waited for a couple more moments, until the Rish seemed to come to some agreement and one dropped down into the hole after Helen. That was it, he could wait no longer; there was no time to come up with a strategy. He must act now or there would be no hope left for Helen.

The group of Rish seemed to come to a new height of excitement as a second of their number leaped down into the hole. There were now only four left above ground. Four was enough, Parenon thought grimly; four was more than enough to tackle at once.

The holva had scattered in different directions and were now standing separately several metres beyond the Rish. As if on a prearranged signal, two of the Rish began walking towards them to herd them back together. Both now had their backs towards Parenon and the other two were still intent on gazing down into the hole. Without taking his eyes off his prey, Parenon crept form his hiding place and behind the first of these. His knife was ready in his hand as he grasped the head of one, lifting up the chin and slashing at the throat. With a sickening gurgling sound the Rish slumped forwards. Before it had even hit the ground Parenon was upon the second, hurling the knife in a sure line towards the evil creature's heart. It found its mark but was deflected by the chains that crossed the front of the Rish's tunic. Maddened with fury it turned on him, rank breath pouring from its mouth as it screamed a warning to its companions.

From the corner of his eye Parenon glimpsed a long spear that had been left on the ground by the hole. He snatched at it and managed to bring it up just in time to strike the Rish before it leapt on him. The speed of its attack, and the weight of its body, drove the spear deep into the creature's belly. It staggered to its knees, clutching at the end of the spear. Parenon twisted it and pushed harder as the Rish let out an agonised scream. This was echoed by other yells and calls from behind him. The other two Rish had been alerted and were hurrying back towards Parenon.

His own knife had skittered away over the hard ground. It was well out of his reach. The Rish on the end of the spear was still alive and snatching at him with two arms, while a third reached for a long sword in its belt. Parenon kept pushing the spear forwards, forcing the Rish back and trying to avoid the flailing arms. The others were now only metres away, he had mere seconds left.

Suddenly, the spear snapped under the pressure and the Rish shot towards him like a missile released from a catapult when the rope is cut. Parenon ducked just in time as the Rish hurtled over his head and into the other two. All three of his attackers ended up in a confused heap, snarling and snapping at each other in rage.

Parenon was upon them in an instant, pulling the Rish's own sword out of its scabbard; he slashed and stabbed with fury until the three bodies lay inert on the ground before him. Breathless and bloody, Parenon threw himself towards the hole after Helen...

The Rish was pulling at Helen's leg, dragging her backwards into the cavern. It almost had her completely back inside now, and she was about to give up her grasp on the outer lip of the opening. There was a scuffling and scrabbling sound behind her. Suddenly through the haze of pain and fear she heard a familiar voice. 'For Mage and Council!' The words were delivered with a finality and cold calm and were immediately followed by a harsh scream as the grip on her leg was relaxed.

As she began to lose consciousness again through the pain, she heard that same familiar voice call her name; felt someone crawling through the crevice next to her; gently taking her hand and softly saying her name over and over. Helen turned to look and there, next to her, was a tall, thin figure in a blue cloak.

'Parenon!'

It was evening. Parenon and Helen were sitting by a glowing fire. Parenon was telling her about how he had managed to rescue her from the Rish. '...they were so intent on trying to find you after you had fallen down into the cavern that at first they did not see me. I had no difficulty jumping down into the cavern. I raced after the final two Rish who were chasing you. Thank Mage and Council that I was in time to rescue you from them.' Parenon reached into his cloak. 'By the way, I found this. I believe it belongs to you.' He handed Helen her missing slipper.

Parenon and Helen were in a cave. It looked out on to the bare plain. Parenon had lit a small fire towards the back of the cave so that the flames would not be seen from the outside. Even though Parenon *had* managed to defeat all the Rish on the plain, they still could not take any chances of being discovered.

After helping her into the cave he had gone out again to hunt for food. He had caught a small creature that Helen thought looked a bit like a rabbit (except for the fact that its fur was blue) and he was roasting it gently over the fire. As the smells wafted over her, Helen realised just how hungry she was. She listened as Parenon continued his story. He went on to tell her his side of what had happened in the battle in the kitchen the night before. 'Was it really only last night?' she kept thinking to herself. So much had happened in the meantime.

Another idea struck her; 'Parenon,' she said, 'it was night-time when we left earth, and daylight when I landed here on Atros. Did it take me the whole night to travel the Pathway?'

'No, your journey would only have taken a matter of minutes at the most,' Parenon answered her. 'The time on Atros is about six hours ahead of earth, and three hours ahead of Beltheron. When it is midnight on earth, it is three o'clock on Beltheron and six o'clock in the morning here.'

'Yes, I had forgotten.' Said Helen. 'Thank you. But tell me what happened next last night.'

'When you ran upstairs with Jack;' Parenon replied; 'your mother and father were right behind you all the time. I was busily engaged in the battle, but I glanced back to the staircase after beheading a particularly ugly Rish – may their souls be skewered in the pits of hell! – and I definitely saw both your parents disappear around the bend in the staircase after you. That was the last I saw of them, because the lights all went out in that moment. However, I managed to throw my luminus into the air so that I could see to fight. I held the Rish back for several minutes. I can only believe that in those minutes your mother and father had enough time to use a Kron to create a Pathway back to Beltheron or to some other haven of safety. Eventually I was overpowered and brought here to this infernal land by those nightmare slaves of Gretton Tur, but until that moment I can promise you that your parents were not pursued. As you managed to follow me here, I assumed that you side-stepped with Jack – that would explain why your parents did not find you upstairs. They must have believed that you had got to safety and so made their own escape. I suppose that you must have then created a pathway of your own to follow me.' Helen nodded to indicate that that was just what had happened.

'At first I just wanted to see where you had gone" she said; 'but the vial didn't seem to work in the way it usually does.'

'Possibly because of the disturbance in the atmosphere created by the Rish's own pathway.'

Helen thought about this. 'Yes, that occurred to me too. Anyway, before I knew what was happening, the Pathway had opened up to follow you and here I am. I just wish I knew that Jack was alright, and where Mum and Dad are.'

'I urge you not to worry.' Parenon continued. 'It is most likely that your parents are much safer than we are at the moment. Jack has the Cleve to looking out for him.'

Helen's face brightened. 'Cleve Harrow is with him?'

'He travelled the Pathway to Jack's house in London several days ago.' Parenon told her. 'He has been watching him ever since. He got onto the same train as Jack and then followed you all from the station to your house yesterday.'

'I haven't seen the Cleve since my last birthday.' Helen interrupted. 'It's a shame he didn't come in to say hello.'

'He had more urgent things to consider. He wished to keep hidden until he was needed. It is just as well, for I am sure he was able to help Jack to safety. The important thing now is for us to find a way to make our own escape from Atros.' Parenon tested the small creature over the fire with the end of a blackened piece of stick. 'His flesh seems tender now. I think it is time to eat him.' Using their fingers, and taking care with the hot meat, they tore it into small strips and stuffed it gratefully into their mouths. Helen thought that it tasted a bit like chicken.

'But how *can* we get back, Parenon?' She spoke between mouthfuls. 'I left my Kron behind, and the vial of liquid I used to follow you got smashed when I travelled through the Pathway.'

Parenon looked thoughtful for a moment. 'That is worrying news. I do not have the power to create a Pathway myself. I would have to use the Golden Staff of Beltheron, and that is with Cleve Harrow.'

He sat in silence, his forehead wrinkling. 'However, we now know that Gretton Tur *is* able to make a Pathway. How else could he transport the Rish to earth?'

Helen too was deep in thought. Parenon spoke again. 'We could always use The Wild Lord's own Pathway to make our escape.' Helen looked up at Parenon sharply, a horrified light dawning on her face.

'I hope you're not about to say what I think you are.'

'I believe I may be, my dear girl.'

'Is there no other way to get back to earth, or to Beltheron?'

'I am only a warrior, Helen, not one of the Select. Without your magic – using the Kron, or that vial of liquid – and without the Golden Staff and Cleve Harrow's spoken permission to use it, I have no way to create a pathway for us. I am afraid that we are trapped on Atros.'

'But couldn't we just wait for someone to come and rescue us?' Helen asked hopefully.

'How would they know which part of Atros to search?' Parenon replied. 'Gretton Tur's Pathway could have transported us anywhere at all.'

'But I was able to follow you.' Chirped up Helen. 'Maybe someone else could find something belonging to one of us and use another vial of liquid to follow us in the same way!'

'You are forgetting just how special your particular gifts are, my dear girl.' Parenon looked down at her affectionately, but with sadness in his eyes. 'You are the only one living, even of the Select, who is able to follow and find people by using the vials. Remember the excitement it caused in the Council, on your seventh birthday, when your gift was discovered?'

Helen did remember. The thought of her mum and dad's expressions of delight and pride on that day came back to her all of a sudden. She dropped her head.

'No,' Parenon continued, 'I am afraid that as far as any rescue party is concerned they have no way of knowing where to look for us. We could be anywhere at all. They do not even know if we are alive or dead and we have no way of contacting them.'

Helen was not going to give up hoping so easily. The thought of her parents had made her more determined again. Her face brightened as another thought occurred to her. 'Someone could follow me using my Kron that I made the Pathway with.'

Parenon answered her with a shake of his head. 'Cleve Harrow could have managed that, but he would have had to have done it by now. The magic that you used would soon have faded. Besides, the only other person in the house was Jack, and he knows nothing of how to use his power.'

Helen sighed as she realised the truth of this.

'So, Parenon continued, 'we can wait here until we are discovered by another group of Rish, or we can take matters into our own hands; we must travel to the lair of the Wild Lord, to the city of Gendrell itself.'

'But wait a minute, Parenon.' There was a frightened, pleading tone in Helen's voice now. She could not believe what Parenon had said. 'That's suicide, surely? The whole reason that Gretton Tur sent the Rish to earth in the first place was to capture Jack and I, wasn't it? So, Tur would just love us to go wandering through Gendrell up to his front door and give ourselves up! He'd laugh his head off… and then probably kill us both!'

'He may not find it as simple as that.' Parenon replied. 'There are more ways of getting into places than just by knocking on the front door. And it is not the first time that I have been to that city.' Helen hoped that he would explain this further. She did not know that Parenon had even been to Atros before, let alone all the way to the dreaded city of Gendrell itself. However, Parenon went straight on: 'We might not be entirely without allies in Gendrell. Our worthy Lord Ungolin also has his agents and spies.'

At the mention of the name of Ungolin, Helen's heart skipped. She had heard the name spoken many times by her mother and father. They always talked of him with respect and awe. Helen had never yet met him in person, but she knew what a great man he was. If someone connected with Lord Ungolin was able to help them, their situation might not be as desperate as she thought.

'Do you mean that Ungolin has spies here, on Atros?' she asked.

'Although it is not openly spoken of, there are whispered rumours of one who is already here. In any case, we cannot just hide out in these caves and on the plains of Atros forever. Gretton Tur is probably already wondering why none of his Rish have returned. He may have sent others along the pathways to search your house on Earth. When the signs of battle are discovered he will know that things have not gone according to his plans. He could be sending out search parties as we speak, and when the bodies of the Rish that I killed today are discovered on the plains below us, then he will know for certain that we are here.' Parenon stood and walked to the entrance to the cave. He gazed out over the plain. From this height he could see a smudge of smoky haze along the horizon to the North. He stood there in silence for over a minute. Then Helen saw his shoulders rise slightly and fall again as he sighed with a sad resolution. He turned back to look directly at her.

'No, Helen. I am afraid that for us to remain here would be the suicide of which you spoke. Both you and Jack are needed *together* in Beltheron. The prophesy tells us so. Not a minute must be lost. We have to be on the move. Our only hope is to look for our ally in the city and seek help there.'

Helen gulped. She turned from Parenon and looked out over the plains to the dark, smoking city far away on the horizon. The city of Gendrell. The very heart of Gretton Tur's domain.

9
In the Great Hall

The Great Hall was one of the oldest buildings in Beltheron City. It had been built over five hundred years ago by the famous architect, Cholus Wheen. Over two thousand stonemasons had worked for twenty five years to complete the main building. There were many of them who had started the job that did not live to see it completed. Even Cholus Wheen himself died tragically, just four days before he was due to lay the final chimney stone at the top of the central tower as part of the grand opening celebrations. He was remembered by a brass plaque on one wall of the Great Hall itself, and honoured by a small golden statue in one of the side rooms where the Council retired to drink their tea during long debates.

The Hall was a solemn place, steeped in history and home to the wisest and most revered people of Beltheron. All of the important decisions in the land's past had been decided in this very room.

As yet however, Jack knew nothing of the rich history of Beltheron, and at the sight of his aunt and uncle, he shouted out in excitement and raced headlong through the crowds to get to them.

'Auntie Jenn! Uncle Matt!' If they were here safely then surely his parents were too! His aunt and uncle stepped towards him, Jenn throwing her arms out as he rushed up to them.

'Jack, thank goodness!'

Uncle Matt slapped him heartily on the back and turned to Harrow, the pleasure on his face mixed with concern. 'Thank you, Cleve, for protecting him...but... Helen?'

Cleve Harrow shook his head, briefly. Jack pulled away from Auntie Jenn to turn to look at the two men. 'You mean, she's not here?'

Matt spoke in a low voice filled with sadness and worry. 'I'm afraid not, Jack. We have not seen her since we followed the two of you up the stairs last night, just before all of the lights went out.'

'It is no surprise to me that she is not here.' Said Harrow. 'She created a pathway to follow Parenon. I am afraid that it now looks as though he was abducted by the Rish and taken to Atros. Therefore, I can only presume that by following him, Helen has also gone there.'

Jack was absorbing this news, and about to ask if anyone had seen his own parents when another voice boomed out at them across the hall. 'Indeed Cleve, I am to your way of thinking. I too believe that the honourable young lady must now be in that vile land.'

The voice was strong and clear. As soon as it began all other sounds in that vast, crowded hall stopped. Jack looked around to try to find who was speaking. The voice continued. 'However, if she is indeed on Atros, we must trust to the fact that she has one of our bravest and best warriors there to protect her. Parenon will lay down his life before allowing anyone to harm her. In the meantime we must decide what is best to be done to secure their safe return to Beltheron.'

Jack saw that the speaker was sitting on a carved wooden chair at one end of the hall. The chair was raised up on a series of platforms, and the man seated there was high above everyone else in the room so that Jack had an excellent view of him.

The man was quite old and decrepit. He was perfectly bald. The top of his head shone bright pink. His limbs were thin and spindly and the cloak he wore looked as if it was too heavy for him and might make him topple over if he tried to stand. And yet his eyes shone with a mischievous sparkle, and there was a dignity about him which struck Jack immediately. The elderly man spoke again.

'Come forward, Master Anders. I have waited a long time to meet you again. You were no more than a babe in arms the last time you were in this room.'

Jack hesitated a moment before stepping forwards. He walked slowly up the whole, long length of the Great Hall, knowing with each step he took that every single pair of eyes in the room was watching him intently. At first he was terribly nervous, and one of the reasons he walked so slowly, was because of the terror he felt at tripping up and making a fool of himself. But as he progressed past the roaring fire in the centre of the Hall, his courage welled up inside him. He strode more quickly up to the base of the platforms where the old man's chair was placed, and bowed down very low. For a moment he remained silent, not knowing what to say in front of such noble company. Then a dignified voice spoke very clearly in the still hush which had fallen over them all. Jack was very surprised to realise that the voice was his own.

'Master Jack Anders,' he said solemnly, 'son of Peter and Sophie, twenty-third generation of the Select Family of Beltheron, greets you my esteemed Lord, and offers his service in the struggle to come.'

Even as he said it he felt his ears burning with embarrassment. What on earth had he been thinking to say something like that? He must have sounded ridiculous! In front of all these people too! What would Orianna think of him? Sure that he had made a complete fool of himself, Jack slowly lifted his head. But to his great relief, instead of an expression of anger or ridicule, he saw the old man gazing down at him with a gentle, fond smile curling at the corners of his mouth. Jack's relief turned to a sudden surge of pride as he realised that at long last he had managed to do something right. Even better, when he turned to look back down the hall to where his companions were standing, he saw Orianna beaming up at him with pleasure. Her smile made his chest feel funny. This made him blush even more, but there was no time to be concerned with that. The Old Lord was rising from his chair, and began to speak.

'Friends. This is a great day. A most important day. For today we see the return of one of our most treasured young men.' In a lower tone he spoke quickly to Jack: 'Come up here my boy and stand next to me.' Jack scrambled up the steps and stood by the old man's chair. The commanding voice boomed out again. 'This boy – as many of you will know – is *Jacques Andresen*.' A huge cheer went up all around the hall. Arms were raised to wave triumphantly at him, and a long, long round of applause echoed up and up to the ceiling. Jack felt quite overwhelmed. The cheering was deafening. Even all those things that he had been told about fulfilling a prophesy, and being of an important family, had not prepared him for this.

'Jacques Andresen!' the old man repeated. Jack wondered for a moment about this strange pronunciation of his name. Then a new fear hit him suddenly in the pit of his stomach. 'Perhaps there's been some mix up,' he thought. 'Maybe this cheering isn't for *me* after all. It's someone else – this *Jacques* person – it's him that they really want.' The expressions on the faces of Harrow, Orianna and the others however, told him that there was no mistake. Jenn and Matt were cheering the hardest of all. Auntie Jenn had tears in her eyes. 'So.' He decided. 'It *is* me that they want then.'

At last, after what seemed like a long time, the cheering and clapping died down. Jack looked up at the old man by his side. The frail figure raised his arms and spoke once more.

'Cleve Harrow, Orianna Melgardes, Matthias and Jenna' – Jack quickly worked out that the last two names must refer to his aunt and uncle – 'must all remain here with Jacques and myself. The five Guardsmen of the Pulver must also remain. All others gathered here must leave us for a while. I need to hold urgent Council!'

He brought his arms down sharply and the doors of the Great Hall swung wide open.

10
Crudpile and Dross

The wooden cart had definitely seen better days. The sides were broken, mostly held together with poorly knotted ropes. The wheels had obviously been taken from other vehicles over the years, they were all different sizes, and caused the cart to wobble dangerously as it travelled along the rutted cinder covered roads. It was pulled by a low, six legged creature that might have been a relative of either a donkey, crocodile, or scorpion. It was difficult to tell, as it shared characteristics with all of them.

The two people leading this sorry looking beast were busy in conversation. They wore brightly coloured jackets, in contrast to the dull, dust-covered shades of their animal and cart. Their breeches were baggy and tucked into brown leather boots, which were laced up to the knee. Wide brimmed hats shielded their eyes from the glare of the sinking sun, directly in front of them on the horizon.

'...an oi tell you there'll be no trouble gettin' into the city as soon as we show them this 'ere in the cart'

'What's in' the cart's exactly the thing wot will be gerrin' us inner trouble. Them Rish'll be wantin' to know jus how two low lifes like us came across the bodies o' some o' their own mates. They'll say we killed 'em, most loike.'

'Shaddup, Dross! What we do is this. We tell 'em the truth – just exactly what we know. We found' a bunch o' their kind murdered on the plain. Signs o' battle. Lootin' an' all that. We tell 'em we brought this'n 'ere to show 'em, to *prove* it, then we sell them information about what else we seen.'

'But we *ain't* seen nothin' else, Crudpile.'

'They don' know that. We make that part of it up, see? Invent a story, stick to it, and sell them the information. Heh, heh, heh! Information that's a bunch o' lies, heh heh!'

'I's not so sure. They're a moighty cruel set o' innivituals up there in Gendrell. Skin the loikes o' us and hang up the skillitins to droi as soon as look at us.'

'Dross! Don't talk so stupit! You'll niver get anywhere wi' thinkin' loike that'.'

'Well what do we tell 'em then? What's our story gonna be?'

'We tell 'em that we've seen eight – no, *twelve*! – wild 'orsemen attack their fellows on the plain; killed them all and their holva, ransacked their bodies an' stole their clothes.'

'But Crudpile, we never saw anythin' of the sort. We just came across those dead Rish bodies lyin' there. There was no one else around. No wild 'orsemen.'

'I know that you oaf! But that don't do us no good do it? We'll just *tell* them that. We'll tell them which way the 'horsemen went, an' what weapons they had. We could even blame it on the rebels in the forest. We know where they are and tellin' the Wild Lord that they done this to his Rish and their holva would increase the reward that's on the rebel's heads. Well tell 'em all this and lots of other information – *for a price*. A heavy rich price, for us!'

A light suddenly dawned on Dross' puzzled face. A gap toothed grin spread across his mouth.

'Ya know Crudpile...it moight jus' work.'

The figures walked on past a mound of rocks and earth at the side of the path. If they had not been so caught up in their own conversation, they might have noticed two more people crouched down behind the rocks. The taller of these two turned and spoke to his young companion.

'Helen, my dear girl, I do believe we have found a way into Gendrell. And if I am not mistaken, some other useful information besides. Follow me and let me do all the talking. Just look terrified. Keep glancing behind you and agree with everything I say.'

Helen had no time to argue. Parenon was already bounding towards the cart.

'Friends! Oh friends! Saviours at last! Oh help us friends, I beg!'

His voice was unnaturally high and he sounded as if he were whimpering from fright. Very different from his real self, Helen thought. The two men with the cart had stopped and were looking at Parenon in amazement.

'Thank you, oh thank you for stopping! Kindest Sirs! We have just witnessed the most terrible slaughter. Many of the noble Gretton Tur's servants have been massacred by twenty giant monsters on the plain! They were riding horses thirty feet high! I have never seen such monsters! We were lucky to escape with our lives. I beg of you, take us into Gendrell where we will be safe. We dare not stay outside the city walls with such creatures around. Imagine! The power to kill so many of the Rish! Just think what they would do to me, or to my young sister here.' He pointed at Helen, who nodded dumbly and tried not to smile at Parenon's intriguing performance.

'Please take us with you into Gendrell.' Parenon continued, breathlessly. 'We have money there, a lot of money. I am a wealthy merchant. I will pay you both handsomely for your help. Gold beyond your wildest dreams, gentlemen!'

Dross and Crudpile looked at each other. Dross

scratched his head and looked confused, but now it was Crudpile's turn to grin widely. His wildest dreams included a very large amount of gold indeed.

'Moy dear friends;' he said, ''how terrible for you. You must be terrified. Of course we will help. Hop up 'ere on the cart an' we'll take you to Gendrell all roight. Money you say? Gold? Well I'm sure we can come to some agreement.'

'Masters, we are so grateful.' Parenon answered in his pleading, whining voice, making Helen want to giggle in spite of herself. Even in the midst of such danger, life with Parenon was always amusing to say the least.

'One other thing;' Parenon continued in a lower tone; 'our business interests sometimes fall on the other side of the law.' He winked broadly at Crudpile, who seemed to be increasingly interested in this odd pair. 'Now I *know* that two such worthy gentlemen of trade, such as yourselves will understand what we mean?'

Crudpile nodded, while Dross was still trying to keep up with this confusing conversation.

'The long and the short of it is,' Parenon went on, 'that our last trade deals fell foul of Gretton Tur. He was angry at us for not declaring all of our vast profits. Now he is searching for us so that he can confiscate...' now Crudpile also looked confused, so Parenon continued; 'erm...*take away* some of our gold. It is vital that we avoid him and his guards in Gendrell. If you can help us to do this, once again a share of our fortune is yours.'

The words 'gold,' 'fortune' and 'share' were all Crudpile needed to hear. Just as Parenon had guessed, this greedy pair of rogues would not think too closely about his rapidly invented story; not if they thought they could get rich quickly without too much effort. Crudpile was already reassuring them and offering his and Dross's help.

'Don' you worry your liddel 'heads over it. You just cloimb up 'ere in the back an' when we get to the city, duck down under them rags there.'

He pointed to the corner of the cart. Parenon leapt up and helped Helen climb onto the unsteady vehicle. The shape of a dead Rish body could be made out under the dirty sheets that Crudpile had pointed to. Helen shuddered at the sight of a long, lifeless arm which stuck out of one corner of the rags. Parenon gripped her shoulder to reassure her and nodded that it would be all right. She huddled into him, partly for the comfort of being near to her friend, and partly to get as far away as possible from the Rish corpse. There was a loud whip crack, and a shouted curse from Crudpile to the poor donkey/ crocodile/scorpion creature pulling the cart. Then, with a sudden rolling lurch they were on their way to Gendrell.

11

A New Plan

In Gendrell itself, the throne room of Gretton Tur's palace stretched out under the flickering light of lamps and torches hung from the walls. Tall pillars of obsidian ran down the sides of the hall and cast long shadows across it. In the centre of the hall, Gretton Tur sat in his usual place on the dark throne. Two figures stepped out of the shadows. Gretton Tur's spies. They stepped forwards and bowed before him.

'What is your news?'

'We now know that the attack on the house failed. The boy escaped with Cleve Harrow. The interfering fool has got hold of him in spite of our efforts.'

'Are you certain that the boy is the chosen one?'

'Yes. It is definitely his image on the Golden Staff.'

Gretton Tur thought for a moment. 'I have means of getting the boy back. We will not fail a second time.'

He made a brief gesture with his right hand. Something moved in the shadows to the side of them. There was a snuffling, sniffing sound. The Wild Lord's spies turned quickly. They peered fearfully into the darkness. What was it? Was Gretton Tur angry with them for their part in the failure of his plans? Were they in danger themselves? The Wild Lord grinned with malice at them both as he read their thoughts.

'Do not panic my faithful ones. I am aware that you

are not to blame.'

He clicked his fingers. The moving shape in the shadows stepped forwards. They gasped as they saw it in the light for the first time. Tur laughed out loud at their discomfort.

The creature was hideous. A lumpen, misshapen slug of a creature. There was no possibility of pity or remorse from this beast. Its heart was cold and unfeeling. It was a Shifter. It had been bred out of malice and hatred to do the Wild Lord's bidding without question.

Four Rish stepped forwards to join the Shifter. By the creature's side, they looked small and insignificant. One of the Rish clasped a small vial of thick liquid in his hand. Another was holding what looked like sheets of brightly coloured, glossy paper. They were folded up together and covered in pictures and words in a variety of sizes and type. It was something that looked so out of place in the Rish's curving hook of a hand that at first it was difficult to understand exactly what this bundle of papers was. The two figures kneeling in front of the throne knew what it was though. It was a film magazine.

'My little pet here will not fail me.' Tur said with a laugh and a gesture towards the Shifter. 'Go now. Go to Beltheron, my beauty, and bring me the boy.'

Gretton Tur raised the Black Staff and pointed it towards them. A shaft of brilliant, white light shot out and enveloped the Rish and the bloated monster. They vanished in a flash leaving behind five burnt scorch marks on the ground.

12

Ungolin's Words

When the doors of the Great Hall of Beltheron swung open, no further signal needed to be given and the huge crowd started to clear. They streamed through the doorways and arches all around the Hall. They moved so swiftly, and with such purpose, that within half a minute the large gathering had almost completely disappeared. However, one figure stepped away from the separating crowds and came towards them. It was a woman, about forty years old. She was dressed very plainly, in a dull green dress made of rough fabric. She walked directly up to Jack, her steely grey eyes piercing straight into his. He took a step backwards, feeling uncomfortable, and a little bit threatened.

'Jacques Andressen,' she said in a kindly voice. He grinned back at her awkwardly – it would take him a while to get used to that pronunciation of his name. It embarrassed him. The woman raised her left arm and placed her hand gently on Jack's cheek. The hand was cool and dry against his face. Jack glanced around at his companions for reassurance. Harrow was smiling back at the stranger and Orianna gazed at her with obvious affection. Jack relaxed again. This woman – whoever she was – was clearly a friend.

'It is good that you are here at last.' The woman said. 'We have waited a long time for you.' She paused and took a deep breath. Jack thought that he could see tears brimming in her eyes.

'You can help us all, Jack. I know that. I know it here in my heart.'

Orianna came forward and put an arm around her, lovingly brushing a few wisps of hair from her forehead. Her head was mostly covered by a shawl and Jack noticed for the first time that the woman's hair was almost exactly the same white as Orianna's. However the stranger's hair also held ageing strands of silver and grey. The woman cupped Orianna's chin in her hands and lifted her head to kiss her. Orianna and the older woman whispered a couple of private words to each other before the woman turned back to Jack, saying; 'I will see you again Jacques, very soon.' She gave a small bow and left them. She was the last person to leave the room. Now only those whom the old man had requested to stay were present. 'Who was that?' Jack asked when she had gone.

'One who has more reason than most to hate the Wild Lord.' Orianna answered him in a strange voice, as if she couldn't quite catch her breath properly. Her head was turned away; she was still watching the woman as she went through a door at the far end of the hall. 'That was Korellia.' Orianna continued. 'She had a son who was taken from her; he was kidnapped by the spies and agents of Gretton Tur when he was still a baby. He has never been seen since.' As she finished speaking, Orianna lifted her hand to her cheek briefly, as if brushing something away. She turned back to face Jack and the Cleve.

He reached towards her and grasped her hand. It was a shock to see her so upset.

'Are you all right, Orianna?' He asked.

She nodded in return and squeezed his hand gently in her own for a moment. 'Yes. Thank you Jack.'

Harrow moved forward towards the platform and

addressed the old man.

'Lord Ungolin, revered Master of the Council, we await your advice and decision in this matter.'

Ungolin stood on his dais and nodded solemnly. He remained silent for a minute, looking around into the faces of the five people standing in front of him. Last of all, his gaze returned to Jack. Ungolin stared deep into Jack's eyes for several moments. Jack felt as if the ancient Lord was peering into his innermost thoughts. It was a very uncomfortable feeling, and he squirmed and dropped his eyes, unable to hold the gaze any longer. Ungolin shook himself briefly, as if he were suddenly waking up, and he began to speak. 'In deference to our young friend Master Andressen here, who, I perceive, has but little knowledge of our situation, allow me to talk for a moment of the ancient days.'

Ungolin paused for a moment and looked at Jack again. He spoke in a friendly tone. 'I am aware that you know little of your true history, Jacques.'

'That's right, Sir.'

'Then hopefully I can fill some of the gaps in your knowledge. When the first generation of the Select was born,' Ungolin continued, 'when the magic in people was strong and pure, a Golden Staff was made. This staff had the power to create Pathways to other worlds; to Earth, where miraculous discoveries and new friends were made, and to Atros, that renegade world of fear and death.'

'Is the Golden Staff the same one that Helen and I are carved into?' Jack piped up. His voice sounded very small and thin in his own ears, after listening to the solemn majesty of Ungolin's speech. 'The same one that Harrow and I used to get here?'

Ungolin nodded. 'The very same, my boy. It is of immense power and untold value to us. Only the Select and their carefully chosen allies have the ability to use the Staff and travel the Pathways, for the permission of the Select was always needed to make the magic of the Golden Staff work. Harrow here often helps us to decide who should be trusted with the privilege of travelling the Pathways. But Gretton Tur the Wild, in his banishment from Beltheron has now created his own Staff – made it for evil uses out of stolen knowledge – and Beltheron and the Earth are in now in the gravest peril. For now He has the power to open up the Pathways. He can send out his devilish Rish, or even return here himself. Who knows how far his cruel imagination will take him on his quest for vengeance?'

Ungolin held everyone's attention in silence for a moment. He looked deeply in turn into everyone's eyes. His solemnity was like a weight on the shoulders of all of them.

'Yes my friends, Gretton Tur's mind is turned to revenge. He has suffered greatly at our hands throughout his long banishment, and now he seeks to make all others quail and suffer also.'

Ungolin paused again before continuing. His brows were furrowed in thought. 'I have considered our course of action over many days and sleepless nights. At first I thought our best hope lay in bringing Jacques and Yelenia together.' (Jack quickly worked out that *Yelenia* must be Helen.) 'We know that their powers are great. We thought that if they could both be brought here, and if they worked together under our protection, then some solution to our troubles might be found.'

'Yes, that is what is suggested by the prophesy.' Cleve Harrow interrupted.

Ungolin silenced him with a brief motion of his hand. He sighed deeply. 'But now all of our plans have been dashed. Now we have lost Yelenia in Gretton Tur's lair.' Jenn gave a small sob and Jack turned to see her hand pressed against her mouth. There was terror in her eyes. She gazed at the ground a few feet in front of her, shaking her head from side to side. Uncle Matt put his arms around her shoulders, but his own eyes were also haunted with fear for his daughter. Ungolin spread his arms towards them both with a comforting gesture.

'My dear, I am sure we will find her. She will be reunited with you and Mathias. And this is how it will be done!'

As he said these words his voice sank to a low whisper. All five of the companions leant forward to hear him. They held their breath as Ungolin continued: 'Cleve Harrow, you will lead a group of Pulver to Atros in order to find Parenon and Yelenia. If Piotre and Sofia have also been captured and transported to Atros – as I now suspect – then you will hopefully find them as well. Jenia and Mathias may also go with you if they wish. 'Jenn and Matt exchanged a brief, relieved glance and reached out for each other's hands. Ungolin turned to Jack. 'You, Jacques, must remain here.'

'No!' Jack shouted. 'That's my mum and dad out there in Atros! I want to go too. I must! You've got to let me try to help!'

Ungolin nodded slowly and went on. 'I understand. It is noble and brave of you, and no more than I would have expected from a Select. But you are too important. You *must* stay here. That is certain. Yelenia is already on Atros. We cannot allow you to risk yourself as well, Jacques, however much I know you wish to do all you can to try to find your mother and father.' He turned to Orianna. 'Orianna Melgardes, for the time being I entrust his safety to you.'

Orianna bowed down very low, her long robes

billowing around her. 'It will be an honour, my Lord.' She said.

Harrow was already talking to Matt and Jenn. They were discussing their imminent journey. 'The Pulver will bring clothing and other tools we will need.' Harrow said, as he beckoned to one of the blue-robed guards who was standing nearby. The Pulver immediately came towards them at a brisk, efficient pace.

'Your orders, Cleve?'

'We will require sturdy boots and warm travelling clothes for all three of us.' Harrow replied. 'I would be most grateful to you, Telenor, if you and five of your most trusted men would accompany us to Atros. I need not remind you of the urgency, importance, and total secrecy of our mission. Lives depend on it. No, it is even more than that. It is not just lives, but our *way of life itself* which is at stake here.'

'Yes Sir. I understand perfectly.' Telenor looked delighted to have been given a part in such a task. He practically glowed as he saluted the Cleve, Matt and Jenn. He then turned, bowed to Ungolin, and walked rapidly towards two of the other guards at one of the entrances to the Great Hall. After a few brief words from Telenor, the three Pulver disappeared quickly through the doorway.

'Now.' Said Cleve Harrow in his most businesslike and commanding tone. 'There is much to do, and not much time to do it in. Orianna, please can you look after Jack until this evening? The three of us will be back here in the Great Hall at seven tonight, before we depart for Atros, we will see you both then.' He lifted his arms towards Jack's aunt and uncle, saying; 'Mathias? Jenia? Shall we go and prepare ourselves?'

Harrow excused himself and walked across the

Great Hall to where another guard stood by a smaller, wooden door.

The others said their brief farewells and followed him. Harrow spoke quickly and urgently to the guard, who nodded, turned and opened the door. Harrow bent his huge frame and squeezed through into the dark corridor beyond. Matt and Jenn, or *Mathias* and *Jenia* as they were called here, followed him.

'Where is he taking them Orianna?'

'There is business that needs to be done before their journey. But if the Cleve himself does not tell you where his business takes him, then sometimes it is better not to ask.'

Jack thought for a moment. 'He's very important, isn't he? I mean, he doesn't shout about it or show off or anything, but I feel he must be.'

Orianna nodded. 'Yes, Jacques. He is very important indeed. Not many people have his knowledge, and he works tirelessly to learn new information. I know that eventually he will help us to defeat the Wild Lord once and for all.'

'He knew Gretton Tur, didn't he?' Jack asked. 'Harrow told me that they were students together.'

'I think he knew him very well, yes. Better than anyone else in those days. They were very close when they were young. He felt Tur's betrayal very deeply. It is a personal grief that he has borne over many years.' They both stood for some moments involved in their own thoughts.

'Come.' Said Orianna at last, her face brightening. 'Let us not become too drawn down and miserable. There are still so many things to hope for. I know that you carry a heavy burden Jack, and your worry for your parents is very great – but let me try to cheer you for a little while. Yes?'

'Uh huh, yes. Thank you.'

'We have a few hours left to our own devices before we are required to return to the Great Hall. I would love to show you more of the city. There is so much to see and do.'

Jack was delighted at the prospect of being able to spend more time with Orianna. It was amazing how quickly she managed to change the serious mood which had threatened to swamp them both. Taking Jack's hand they ran together towards the far end of the Great Hall and down corridors and stairways, under the watchful eyes of the guards.

13
The Shifter

'This is a good day to be seeing the city.' Orianna told Jack. 'It is a market day and a feast day combined. There will be many fascinating sights.'

There were indeed. Living in London, Jack was used to busy streets and crowds of people. He was also used to seeing a wide variety of cultures and assorted styles of architecture from different periods of history all together. In spite of this, Beltheron took his breath away. Orianna led him through high, carved archways and past decorative fountains. Jack began to think that he had never seen a city that was more beautiful and enthralling. Blue and Yellow flags had been unfurled from the pinnacles of many of the towers, and were flapping from the windows of dozens of inns and domestic houses as they passed.

'Those flags are for the Feast Day.' Orianna explained. 'Today we are celebrating the anniversary of the Witch Queen's creation of the Council five hundred and fifty years ago.' The two of them ran towards the Central Square. Jack's head spun around, trying not to miss any of the enthralling sights.

The bright sun was now well past the mid-day arrows that pointed up from the Time Tower in the middle of the Central Square of Beltheron. Orianna pointed it out to Jack as they walked beneath a wide, yellow brick archway and came in full view of it. The Time Tower, she explained to him, was an ingenious invention. Partly a civic building (it housed many offices, libraries and studios) partly a sculpture and partly a clock, it was the initial idea of the same architect, Cholus Wheen, who had designed the Great Hall. Wheen soon realised however, that he did not have the technical abilities to carry his idea to fruition. Instead he hired a scientist and a member of the Select – one of Jack's very own ancestors – to combine their knowledge and power in order to build it. The Tower itself was made of silver metal with twelve massive glass rods radiating outwards from the top. These rods caught and reflected the sun's light. But that was not the clever part. The light and the heat gathered in the rods were conducted down the tower through brass and silver tubes. In this way the Time Tower generated the heating for the whole of the building. But that was not the clever part. Over the whole of Beltheron City an intricate network of twenty three mirrors reflected the light of the rods and shone onto twenty three different sundials. But that was not the clever part. Twenty three tiny motors, each one powered by the reflected light shining onto its own mirror continuously adjusted the mirrors into a preset series of positions so that the light shining on the twenty three sundials, all coming originally from the sun, was always at exactly the right angle so that every sundial told the correct time every minute of the day. And *that* was the clever part.

'You will notice that I said there were twenty three sundials?' Orianna said to him as she finished her explanation.

'Yes,' Jack replied, 'but I thought that there might have been twenty four. One for each hour of the day.'

'The sundials do not commemorate the hours of the day. They are to celebrate something else Jack.'

He thought about the number twenty three again

and grinned as he realised the connection. 'There are twenty three because Helen and I are twenty third generation Select!'

Orianna laughed with him. 'Yes, one is added for each new generation of your noble family. When you or Helen have children of your own another sundial with its own set of mirrors will be added, somewhere in the city.'

They walked on, chattering easily with each other. Orianna had other things to show him, and other stories to tell of the fascinating city that she obviously loved.

They continued walking across piazzas and wide sunny streets. The blue and yellow flags were everywhere and many children ran past them, laughing and calling out to one another, with their faces painted in the same colours. For the first time Jack realised that the blue was the same shade as the colour of Parenon's cloak.

He was about to ask Orianna if this had any significance when they turned a corner, into another, narrower street. There his attention was distracted by another of the strange floating buggies which buzzed past at about head height. Jack was still fascinated by these machines – especially up close. They were all so very different. He spun around to look as it hovered at the road junction. This one was shaped like an inflatable rubber ring and the driver sat on the edge, moving the controls in front of him, with his legs dangling over the side.

'Weird,' thought Jack, 'if I had one of those things, I would want it to look like a motor bike, or a space ship.' He watched as the man sped away on his rubber ring. Then he smiled to himself as he realised that, in a way, these strange things *were* space ships.

Another one flew over his head. It must have reflected the sunlight as a bright glaring flash of red blinded Jack for a moment as he looked at it.

He blinked to clear his vision again and saw that Orianna had walked on ahead of him while he had been engrossed with watching the flying machines. He was about to turn back to run after her, when he saw a familiar face in the group of people across the street. It was one of the guards from the Great Hall; the one who had first spoken to Cleve Harrow. Jack began to raise his hand to wave. Then something strange happened. The man had been looking straight at Jack, but as soon as their eyes met, the guard looked away and began walking in a different direction down the street.

'That's funny,' Jack thought, 'I wonder if he's been sent by Harrow to keep an eye on us?' It was odd the way he had turned away though. Jack was puzzled. 'I'd better tell Orianna.' There she was, walking down the street around the corner from where he had stopped just a few moments ago to watch the flying buggy. She was peering around anxiously for him. A look of relief flashed across her face as soon as she saw him.

'Try to keep up Jack. I don't want to lose you!'

'Orianna, I just saw something that – well – it's probably nothing but…' he paused, unsure now of what he thought he had seen.

'Go on Jack' Orianna urged. 'Tell me, whatever it was.'

'Well, just now I thought I saw that guard from the Hall. The one who spoke to us at the door. Callan…er, Canning…'

'Cannish?'

'Yes, him. He was watching me, over there. But then I saw him and he hurried off – no! Look! There he is again!'

Orianna spun around in the direction Jack was pointing.

Walking swiftly towards them was the figure of

Cannish. He strode purposefully across the street. But about half way across he seemed to shudder, and his face rippled, as if his skin was a pool of water and someone had thrown a small pebble into it.

Orianna's face had set into a hard serious expression. Her eyes darted around the street and she gripped Jack's arm. 'Well spotted Jack,' she said in a low, urgent voice. 'Come, we had better leave here, and quickly. Follow me.'

Pulling Jack after her, she hurried off the main street and down a short alleyway. At the other end they came out into a large town square, with another of the Time Tower's sundials raised up on a platform in the middle. They both turned together and looked behind them. The guard was still following, and getting nearer. Walking rapidly into the crowd of people, Orianna pushed Jack along in front of her so quickly that he had to break into a trot. They bumped into a large man waving a flag in one hand and carrying a large bottle of beer in the other. He grinned drunkenly at them. 'Harpy feshtival!'

'And to you, sir.' Orianna ducked under his arm and grabbed Jack's hand to follow her.

'Come, we might lose him in this crowd.'

'Orianna, what's the matter? 'Do you think Cannish is the spy?'

'No Jack, I think the spy who betrayed you would have to be more highly placed than one of the Guards of the Great Hall.'

'So why don't you trust Cannish, Orianna? Why do we have to run?'

'Because, Jack, that's not Cannish.'

'What?' Jack didn't know what Orianna was talking about. 'It *was* him, Orianna, I'm sure of it. It looked just like him.'

'It looked like him to be sure, but what you really saw

was a Shifter.'

'A Shifter?'

'A creature that can change its shape at will. It can make itself look like whatever it chooses.'

'And I'm guessing that they're not on our side, right?'

'No Jack, they work with the Rish in the service of the Wild Lord. I have read about them, but this is the first time I have ever seen one.'

They had ducked into an alleyway and through to another square filled with people. Orianna pushed on as quickly as she could.

'So how can you be so sure that it *was* a Shifter, and not Cannish?'

'Did you see the way his skin moved? The way his face rippled?'

Jack looked puzzled for a moment, then nodded.

'That's a sure sign.' Orianna continued. 'They form an image of whatever they want to appear as, but they can't keep that image steady all the time. It takes an immense amount of energy.'

They were almost across the square now. She glanced back. The figure following them had only just come out of the last alleyway and into the square. It gazed around, trying to find them in the crowds.

'In here.' They ducked into a doorway that was set far enough back from the main thoroughfare to hide them in its shadow. Orianna tried the rusty metal handle. It rattled under her hand but the door wouldn't budge. 'Locked' she said. 'Jack, do you have the Kron?'

'Yes, it's here.' Jack fumbled in his pocket and brought out the glowing ball that Harrow had given him. 'You must use it Jack.' She spoke quickly, breathlessly, and Jack could feel his own fear and tension increase as he realised that she too was frightened.

'I do not have the power,' Orianna continued, 'but you – as a twenty third generation Select – do. Have you Sidestepped before?'

'Yes, once, the other night. With Helen – but *she* made the Kron work, Orianna, not me. I don't think I know how.'

Orianna peered briefly around the arch of the doorway, back into the street. She immediately pulled her head in again.

'Now would be a good time to try,' she whispered, 'the Shifter is coming this way.'

'O.K.' Jack tried to remember what had happened when Helen had used her own Kron. 'Put your hands over mine on the Kron' he instructed Orianna. 'Now breathe in deeply, at the same time as me, and then let it all out of your lungs as slowly as you can.' She followed his instructions. Jack just hoped that he was getting it right. They breathed out together, clutching the Kron. This was just what he had done with Helen, he was certain. He was almost out of breath, and Orianna was nodding to tell him she too was nearly ready. What had Helen done next? It seemed that she had just tossed the Kron into the air. With one last inquiring look at Orianna, he did so. The ball dropped back into his hand. Nothing happened. He looked at Orianna desperately. She smiled encouragement back. He focused all his attention on the Kron, staring at it hard. Biting his lip with anxiety, he tossed the ball into the air again. Nothing.

'I'm so sorry Orianna, I just *can't*…'

'Hush!'

She pulled him into the corner of the doorway. They both squeezed as far back into the shadows as they could. Jack could hear the steps of the Shifter drawing closer down the alley along the side of the buildings towards them. They both clung to each other. Orianna's hand tightened around his arm. The slowly pacing steps came closer and closer. Now even the creature's rasping breathing could be heard; it seemed to be pausing every few steps. 'It's looking into all the doorways!' Jack realised with horror; 'it knows that we're here somewhere and its searching! It doesn't matter how dark it is in here, or how far back we squeeze into this corner, it's bound to find us!'

Then a strange sensation swept over Jack. He had a sudden, clear memory of knotted cords untying under his fingers, and heard Cleve Harrow's voice in his head, 'just one of your gifts my dear boy.' Without really knowing why, Jack moved his hand to the locked door handle behind them. He closed his fingers around it and with hardly any effort at all, the handle moved and the door swung open. The Shifter must now be no more than two or three paces away. Jack could hear its rasping breathing much louder now. He pushed Orianna backwards through the opening. He stepped in quickly behind her and closed the door as silently as he could. They paused behind it, breathless with fright. The very next moment they heard a scuffling, sniffing sound from outside. 'What if it can smell us?' thought Jack. They both stood perfectly still. Every nerve in Jack's body seemed to be stretching out as he listened… listened…listened.

There was one more loud sniff, and then the scuffling stopped and the footsteps moved away.

They breathed a huge sigh of relief.

'We had better wait here for a minute. We must make sure the Shifter has indeed gone away.'

Jack nodded. 'Absolutely, Orianna, whatever you say.' He was more than happy to stay exactly where he was. At that moment he thought he wouldn't mind if he never had to step outside into such a mad and dangerous world ever again.

Orianna held up her hand to touch the door. 'Well done for thinking of using your power on the door, Jack.'

'I didn't even know if it would work. I was so angry with myself for not being able to use the Kron, but then the idea just came to me. It was as if something inside was telling me I could open a locked door if I just touched it.' He told Orianna about how he had undone the knots tying Harrow's bag together. She frowned, fascinated, and concentrated hard on what he said.

'That is a skill that I have not heard of before. It is certainly nothing that the Cleve has ever told me about in any of my studies. It is obviously one of your own special powers, Jack.' She smiled, admiration and delight written across her face. 'Who knows? It may be a gift which is unique to you.'

'At least I can do *something*.' Jack replied.

'Do not be too hard on yourself. Maybe the Kron didn't work because *I* am not Select. It might not have had anything to do with you getting it wrong. And remember, that you still managed to save us both.' She really was very kind. With just those few words she had made him feel a lot better. Yes! He had saved them! He grinned. He had saved Orianna Melgardes from a Shifter! But there were so many other things that he knew he would have no power against. He felt so comfortable talking to Orianna, however that he continued chattering on in a rush, without any embarrassment: 'to tell you the truth, Orianna, I feel completely out of my depth. So many people here expect so much of me. Helen and I are supposed to be the saviours of the land, the only hope for Beltheron. But without you and Harrow I'd be completely lost. Even as it is, I haven't a clue about what I should be doing.' He looked down at his hand which still held the Kron. His happiness of a few moments ago disappeared completely. 'I can't even get this stupid thing to work.'

'And that is why we are here. To help you. Until you discover what you *can* do. None of us know exactly what your part in all this will be.' She looked seriously at him. 'But your role will be vitally important, whatever it is. I am sure of it, Jack, and for what it is worth, I have every faith in you.'

He didn't know what to say. He couldn't even look her in the eyes. His parents had never given him any responsibility. As far as he could remember, they had never told him that they had faith in him, or were proud of him. He dropped his head. 'Thank you' he mumbled. 'I'll try not to let you down. I promise.'

Orianna sensed his embarrassment. 'Come. It should be safe out there by now, let us check.'

Cautiously she moved to the door and tried to turn the handle. Laughing, she stepped back, 'Guess what? It's locked again! You had better open it for us Jack.'

He did so without difficulty. He was starting to enjoy this. They stepped outside into the sunlight. They both checked carefully, but neither of them could see the shape of Cannish anywhere. 'Come on,' said Orianna, 'it looks safe enough now.'

A thought occurred to Jack. 'Orianna?'

'Yes?'

'How long does it take a Shifter to change shape?'

'I'm not sure, but not long I don't think.'

'And a Shifter can change into the shape of anything it likes?'

'Yes I suppo...' Orianna's mouth dropped open. 'I see what you mean. Of course! How foolish of me! The Shifter could still be around; it could have changed into anything or anyone at all! Come, there is somewhere not far from here where we can go.'

They sped back across the square in the direction they had first come. Neither of them saw the figure of a tall elegantly dressed woman following them, or the way that her skin rippled slightly in the light as she moved.

14
Into the Enemy's Lair

Helen and Parenon rattled around on the back of the cart. The towers of Gendrell rose up in front of them. They were now very close to the vast black stone wall which surrounded the dread city. An immense pair of rusted iron gates lay directly in front of them. There were other, smaller doors around the wall, each one barred by heavy chains and padlocks. 'I would guess that they are the quarters for the city guards and the soldiery.' Parenon whispered into Helen's ear.

'Nearly there now' Dross called to them from in front of the cart where he was leading the donkey, crocodile, scorpion creature.

Parenon jumped down from the cart and trotted to catch up with him.

'Remember what we said, my dear sir? It is vital that Tur does not know we are here.'

'Don' worry, get back in an' we'll hide you under the rags.'

They did so. The harsh material stank, and Helen was sure she could feel the dead claw of one of the Rish bodies scratching her arm. She shivered.

The cart rumbled on for another couple of minutes. It suddenly got much colder. Helen realised that they must be passing under the shadows of the city walls. Another long, suspenseful minute dragged by and then a voice could be heard from up ahead.

'You there! Yes you! Halt!'

Crudpile's voice replied. 'Us Sir? Yes Sir, whatever you say.'

The sickening motion of the cart ground to a stop. Helen held her breath. The first voice continued.

'Who are you two ugly mugs, and what is the purpose of your visit to Atros?'

'We carry goods to trade in your markets sir. We are regular visitors to your city.'

'Goods? What sort of goods?'

Helen flinched as she heard the voice moving around towards her side of the cart.

'What is it you carry under these rags?'

A heavy stick came crashing down on top of the rough fabric and landed on Parenon's leg. He tightened his grip around Helen's hand, but made no other move. Helen felt her heart hammering in her chest so loudly that she was sure the Atros guard would hear it.

'Please, Sir!' Crudpile's voice was quick and pleading. 'Do not do that! Lord Gretton Tur would not take kindly to you damaging his things!'

There was a very brief silence while the guard summed up this new information.

'The Wild Lord's things? You have goods for the Wild Lord?'

'Indeed,' Crudpile continued. 'We often find items of interest for 'im, don't we Dross?'

Parenon and Helen heard Dross give a grunt of agreement, and both silently thanked Crudpile for his surprisingly quick thinking.

'And if you spoil our latest find, one of great interest to Gretton Tur, then I am sure 'e would be most unpleased, oi mean, erm... dis-happy, ur, ANGRY with you!!'

There was another, much longer silence.

'Very well.' Said the guard's voice at last. 'Carry on your way.'

'Thank you, Sir. Oi won't forget this.'

The cart resumed its slow, creaking motion forwards through the gates and into the City itself.

Helen's bruises ached with every stone and crevice that the cart rumbled over. It was getting hotter and stuffier under their covers all the time, and the rotting stench from the Rish carcasses was beginning to make them both gag and retch. Then, at long last, after many twists and turns, the cart slowed once more and stopped. There were no sounds of the city outside now. All was deathly quiet. Parenon was about to raise a corner of the rags with his hand in order to peer out when suddenly the rags were pulled back with a violent jerk. Crudpile's face leered at them. Both he and Dross were grinning mercilessly and Helen saw that they held heavy cudgels in their hands. Crudpile spoke first, a sliver of grey drool spilling from the corner of his mouth and running in a slow, sickening river down his thin jaw.

'Right. Fun's over. You've 'ad your ride. Now get out!'

'Sirs, we are mightily grateful for...' Parenon began, but he was interrupted by Crudpile. His tone of voice and his whole manner towards them had changed. He pointed his cudgel directly at Parenon.

'Shut up! Get out of the cart. Slowly now – I don't want any sudden moves.'

Parenon kept up his pretence of being a nervous, wary merchant. 'My dear Sirs, is there anything wrong? Have we reached safety? Oh how I pray that you have delivered us to safety.'

'Quiet!' Roared Crudpile. 'Oi won't tell you again!'

he was swinging his cudgel lightly back and forth in his hands, only centimetres from Parenon's face.

'You must think that I'm a real idiot. Did you really expect me to believe a ridiculous story loike yours? Eh? You didn't fool me for a minute with your 'merchant' this and 'reward' that. Oi keep my ear to the ground and my eyes wide open. Oi know what goes on in Gendrell, and oi know oi ain't seen the likes of you two before. Gretton Tur pays very well for information, especially these days, and he pays even better for prisoners. Oi reckon that yew belong to one of them rebel gangs as is being talked about.'

'Rebels, sir?' Parenon interrupted, trying to stall for time. 'I can assure you that we don't...'

'Quiet!' Crudpile was obviously in no mood for any more foolery. 'That's right, Rebels. At first I thought they was just a rumour, but Dross and me saw some of them last month. Out in the wilds they live, in the woods to the North of the City. We listened in to 'em for ages. One of 'em was called Tarawen and it seemed they all answered to 'him. They was plotting and planning against Gretton Tur. You two belong to them rebels all right and there's no use denying it! That Tarawen is probably payin' you to spy for 'him. Now Dross and me have got a *real* reward comin' our way. The Wild Lord'll be well pleased with two rebel spy prisoners. Now Gerrout of the cart!' his voice rose to an ugly scream. He now seemed like a very different person to the one they had first encountered only a few hours ago.

Helen looked at Parenon, wondering if he had any plan but he merely shook his head slightly, and began to climb down out of the back of the cart. Crudpile held his weapon steady, still very close to Parenon's head. Dross giggled in a high sickening whinny. Helen thought he sounded like one of her friend's mean-spirited ponies that she had once ridden at home. How far away that all seemed to her now! It was looking very doubtful that she would ride a horse, or see any of her friends ever again. Parenon held out his hand to her and helped her down. Her twisted leg buckled under her as she put her weight on it and she cried out sharply. She had obviously hurt herself more than she had at first thought when she had been running from the Rish. Parenon's hand shot out and held her arm, supporting her so that she did not have to use her injured leg.

'Careful!' Crudpile snapped. 'I said no quick moves.'

'She is hurt you slobbering imbecile.' Parenon retorted. All of his pretence and character acting had now gone, replaced by his keen anger. How dare these two villains treat the Lady Yelenia like that? He spoke slowly, spitting each word out into Crudpile's face. 'I will help her in any way I can and you will not stop me with your ridiculous threats.' His voice now held more menace in it than Helen thought she had ever heard before. Crudpile was about to reply, but Parenon continued. 'Now – you miserable excuse for a dung-rat's breakfast! If you so much as touch one hair on her head, I assure you that I will knock that club from your hand and kill you so fast that you will be dead before it even hits the floor.'

Crudpile and Dross turned to look at each other.

'Oi think we should hand 'em over as corpses,' said Dross.

'Yur, especially *this* one.' Crudpile added, jerking his head in Parenon's direction. 'There's bound to be a reward for 'em, whether they're alive or not!'

The two of them grinned widely at each other and raised their clubs over their heads to attack.

In a blur of movement, Parenon shot forwards between them and under their arms. As he moved, his fists punched sharply upwards, connecting with both of their jaws and snapping back their heads. Before either Dross or Crudpile could even cry out, Parenon had spun around again and disarmed the pair of them. He booted Dross in the backside with his left foot so that he staggered into the cart. Then he swung Crudpile's own club at his head, knocking him to the ground in an unconscious heap. The whole thing had only taken two or three seconds, and Parenon had realised his victory over the two thugs in almost complete silence.

He and Helen now looked around them for the first time. Helen recognised the type of building straight away. They had been brought into some kind of stables. It had a high, beamed ceiling and two long rows of stalls for horses or cattle running down either side. The stalls were all empty. There were no animals, and no other people there.

Parenon broke the silence. 'Quickly Helen. This way!'

She limped towards him.

'Parenon, I don't think I can run very far. I'm not sure that I can even walk.'

'Let me help you.' He swung her up into his arms. In this way they crept down the centre of the stables to an oak door at the far end.

'Can you stand for a moment while I open the door?' Parenon asked.

Helen nodded. 'Yes I think so.'

He lowered her gently to the ground. Helen gingerly placed her injured foot on the uneven surface. She staggered a moment but then managed to support herself with one hand on the wall next to her.

The door had a huge brass handle, worn and rusty with use and old age. Parenon twisted it with both hands and with a groan the door swung open. When they walked outside they found themselves in a deserted alleyway. Parenon glanced up and down the alley briefly, and then swung Helen up over his shoulder into a piggy back. She clung on as he turned left and began to walk towards a larger street at the end of the alleyway.

'Where do we go now?' Helen asked him.

'Not into Tur's lair as I first suggested.' He replied. 'From what we heard from those two fools back there,' he jerked his head back in the direction of the stables, 'I think it would be more profitable for us to find the camp of rebels, join them and seek their help.'

'Do you think we can trust them? The rebels I mean?'

'They were obviously enemies of Dross and Crudpile. They feared this man Tarawen and his followers. That in itself makes me feel safer in their company than on our own.'

Parenon hoisted Helen a little higher onto his shoulders.

'One thing is certain though,' he continued. 'I cannot carry you like this through the city indefinitely. We need to find horses.'

'I think that I could ride, even with my foot.' Helen sounded apologetic, and in her mind she was repeating to herself, 'stupid, stupid, stupid!'

They were approaching the end of the alleyway now. There was more noise coming from a low building on the other side of the main street. A dull, yellow light came from the small grimy windows and the shouts, raised voices and occasional drunken laughter suggested to Parenon that the building was some kind of alehouse. There were a variety of men and several bizarre creatures walking and riding up and down the street. Some two or three hundred metres up the street on his left, he saw the large wooden gateway through which Dross and Crudpile had led them earlier.

To his dismay, Parenon saw that now there were also three Rish on their hideous Holva steeds guarding the gateway as well as the sentry who had let their cart through. Had the Rish been alerted? Did they suspect anything? Parenon was certain that he did not want to fight his way out of the gates, even on horseback. And he knew that Helen could not ride far in her injured, exhausted state. He had to find some sort of transport for them both, and come up with a diversion. But what?

15
Vishan

Over the years, Vishan had been on many expeditions and adventures for the Cleve. He was a Pulver captain, one of the bravest and most respected soldiers in Ungolin's army. He had trained as a young man alongside Parenon and the guard Cannish, and led them into battle against the forces of the Wild Lord on many occasions. But Vishan was not only a brave fighter, he was adept at all kinds of tracking, espionage and disguise. He often travelled the Pathway to Atros. Cleve Harrow sent him to the Rish Caverns outside the City walls of Gendrell. Here he would hide out and listen to what the Rish were planning, and report back to Harrow. This mission though, was different. It was the first time that he had been sent down into the city of Gendrell itself. Harrow needed precise information, as much as he could gather, of the layout of the Wild Lord's city. Vishan's memory was precise and exact. He could recall a place or a person from long ago and describe them down to the smallest detail. From just a few coded notes and scribbled lines to help, his memory of a long, complex overheard conversation was total. Cleve Harrow had never known Vishan to let him down.

This fantastic memory, which made Vishan such a valuable spy, also made him vulnerable. He carried so much information in his head that his loss or capture would be a heavy blow. Perhaps it was dangerous then, for Harrow to send him on a mission into the very heart of his enemies? Vishan knew the risks and he accepted them. He had sworn fealty to Ungolin and to the cause against Gretton Tur. He had every reason not to betray them. His hatred of Gretton Tur and the Rish was total. He would die before he revealed his knowledge to them, or put any of his friends and colleagues in danger. Vishan did not fear death. His only fear was failure against the evil power of the Wild Lord.

The Pathway had transported Vishan to the woods on the outskirts of the city. It had taken him the best part of the night to approach the city walls and scale them without being seen by any of the guarding Rish who patrolled the battlements. As the first light of dawn crept up over the walls and lit up the dirty streets of Gendrell, he was huddled over a fire, disguised in tattered rags, just one of the many dispossessed souls who lived in the alleyways. No one was taking any notice of him and he appeared to be taking no notice of anything going on around him. Vishan was in fact alert to the slightest thing. His eyes were fixed most of all on the large gateway which led into the higher levels of the city. These gates gave access to the paths and roads up to the palace of Gretton Tur himself. At some point in the day, these doors would open. Then Vishan could take his chance. Then he could break into the innermost circle of the city.

Most of the morning went by with no activity at all, but Vishan was patient. He could wait for as long as it took. He knew how important it was for him to get through those gates. He had already discovered that Gretton Tur was able to create pathways of his own, but only a week ago he had discovered something even more worrying. The Wild Lord could now follow and find a particular person using a similar process to that used by the Lady Yelenia. Vishan had found a vial of liquid and overheard a conversation which led him to believe that the Cleve must act quickly to avert disaster.

Vishan knew, as well as Harrow and Orianna Melgardes did, that if the Wild Lord had managed to fashion a vial and use it with such skill then the knowledge must have come from an informer, or informers, with a great deal of power themselves. Like many good spies, Vishan suspected everyone until their absolute trust and fidelity had been firmly established. He had to be suspicious. That is what had kept him alive for so long in such a dangerous and secretive business.

Now it was time for him to make a move. He gathered the ragged clothes of his disguise around him and stood up. The streets were already beginning to get busier, with Gretton Tur's troops already starting to mobilise around the town. They had been getting more and more active recently, Vishan had noticed. It looked as if a big military strike was being planned. Another reason that he should not fail in his task to gain useful information, he thought to himself grimly.

As he made his way through streets that were gradually becoming familiar to him, he caught sight of something unusual. A young girl was hobbling along on the arm of a man. He was dressed in a bright blue cloak with high leather boots and a long sword at his side, whilst the girl looked as if she was wearing a robe tied around the middle, with a baggy, patterned cotton garment underneath. Amongst the dark and ugly clothing of most of the rest of the inhabitants of Atros City, these two looked quite out of place.

Vishan looked again and suddenly grinned with recognition. He hurried across the dirty cobbles, dodging a line of sorrowful looking prisoners being led on a chain by a large Rish. It turned to him as he stepped in its way and snarled angrily. The blank, dark eye slits glared at him and one of its upper arms pushed him out of the way. Then it yanked on the chain and continued on its way, the prisoners staggering behind it. Vishan returned to his pursuit.

The two figures that he was following had ducked into a side alley. He picked up his pace so as not to lose them. Running into the alley he saw them again up ahead. They had stopped and were looking all around anxiously. Vishan realised why. They had come to a dead end.

Vishan glanced behind to make sure that he was not being followed into the alley. Everything seemed clear. He walked towards them, starting to speak rapidly before he even got too close.

'Mage and Council protect you both. I beg you not to be alarmed. I am a friend. I can help.'

Parenon (for of course it was he) spun around. He dropped into a fighting crouch. He straightened immediately as soon as he saw Vishan.

'My friend!' he laughed. 'What a relief to see you! Your help would certainly be helpful. We need to get out of Gendrell as quickly as possible.'

'Then follow me. I can certainly aid you in that.'

Vishan led them down the street. Whenever they could they ducked into doorways so that Vishan had the chance to look up and down the street; as far as he could tell, they were not being followed.

Their route took them by many turnings and – as it seemed to Helen – they doubled back on themselves several times until they finally reached a dirty, black-bricked building with a low fabric awning overhanging the road. A sign hung down from a rusty bracket on the wall by the door. As they drew nearer, Helen looked up and saw the carving on the sign. She shuddered. It was the image of a Holva steed with a Rish upon its back. The Rish was swinging a hideous looking scythe down towards a small furry animal on the ground. The animal looked a bit like a cat. The Holva had one of its skeletal hooves on the cat's tail. Underneath this image were carved the words: 'The Hunter and Holva.' The doorway itself had another smaller sign above it. It simply said 'Bar'. The door was open but it was dark inside. A stale stench reached Helen's nostrils. The whole place looked disreputable and dangerous.

Vishan saw the doubt in Helen's face as it became obvious that they were going in.

'Don't worry.' He said. 'The people in this inn know me. They are a mixed bunch of brigands, thieves and cut-throats. They would sell their own brother to the Wild Lord for the price of a drink, but I have done enough of them favours in the past. They have a grudging respect for me. Those that are with me are as safe in 'The Hunter and Holva' as anywhere else in this accursed city.'

Vishan went in first. Parenon followed close behind with his arm wrapped protectively around Helen's shoulder.

Inside the smell was much worse. It was like a mixture of boiled cabbage and old ashtrays filled with cigarettes ends. Helen gagged and held her hand to her mouth.

Their eyes gradually grew more used to the dim light and she and Parenon became aware of a number of figures sitting around at low tables, huddled over drinks. Several more stood at the bar at the far end of the room. They were lit more clearly by a lamp that hung from the ceiling and from a couple of black candles on the bar. These threw a yellow glow over the grim faces. Vishan was making his way towards one of the figures at the bar.

'Come on,' Parenon whispered to Helen, 'I think that we had better stay with our new friend.'

Helen just nodded, then swallowed hard. Vishan's

friends or not, these people were frightening. One or two of them turned to look at her and Parenon. She hoped that none of them could hear her heart hammering in her chest.

Vishan reached the bar and threw some coins down onto it. 'Ragosh!'

A large, bearded man at the far side of the bar looked up from where he had been wiping a glass with a greasy cloth. He stared at Vishan; his mouth opened into a wide grin.

'Hello there stranger! It's been over a month. What trouble have you been getting yourself up to then eh?'

'Nothing that could bring a worse reputation to the 'Hunter and Holva' than it already deserves.' Vishan laughed in return. 'Now, you torn piece of nose wipe, stop lounging about making the place look untidy and get me my usual.'

Ragosh laughed out loud. 'Your manners don't improve with age, do they Vishan?' He made his way towards them, reaching for a bottle as he did so. 'I swear, if you weren't a good customer, with money to spend...'

'...You would still recognise my strength and short temper and serve me anyway.' Vishan finished for him. Now everyone at the bar laughed. Helen and Parenon both relaxed a little. It was obvious that Vishan knew what he was doing. He did seem to have a strange respect amongst the drinkers at 'The Hunter and Holva'.

'And get two more for my friends here.'

Their drinks were poured and handed to them. Helen couldn't help thinking of the greasy scrap of cloth that Ragosh had been wiping the glasses with when they came in. She took her drink and looked at it suspiciously. It was bright green and foaming. The foam gave off a strange steam that smelt of petrol. Vishan and Parenon had already taken large gulps out of their drinks. Parenon's eyelid flickered as he swallowed, but he made no other sign of distaste. Vishan downed the rest of his in a single swallow and banged his empty glass back down on the bar. 'Another round of those, and then a word with you, Ragosh.' He said.

Helen raised her glass to her lips and took a sip. The liquid was thick and oily on her tongue. There were small gritty pieces in it that grated against her teeth. It made her think of out-of-date cough mixture and toilet cleaner. It was all she could do not to throw up on the spot. 'People drink this for fun?' she thought to herself disbelievingly.

They moved towards a table in one of the darker corners of the inn. After serving a hooded creature with wiry hair covering its face and only one eye in the middle of its forehead, Ragosh came around the bar to join them. He sat between Parenon and Helen, who still hadn't summoned up the courage to take another sip of her drink.

'Right then Vishan, you old villain, what do you want from me?'

'Your cellar. Or to be more precise, the thing under your cellar.'

Ragosh's eyes gleamed. He loved intrigue and Vishan could always be relied upon to provide it.

'Any time, Vishan, any time at all for you. For the usual price of course.'

'Of course.'

Vishan's hand went to his pocket. He drew out a handful of coins and passed them under the table to Ragosh.

'Wait a couple of minutes and then follow me behind the bar.' Ragosh got to his feet. He made his way around a couple of the other tables, collecting glasses and saying a few words to his other customers before making his way back to the bar.

Vishan spoke to his friends. 'There is a secret tunnel underneath this inn. I have used it myself in the past to escape capture. It leads you out on the north side of the city. The tunnel is dark and it stinks, but the worst that you will encounter down there are a few rats. They will probably be more scared than you are.'

Parenon nodded. 'Thank you Vishan. When we are outside the city we need to find our way to the rebel camp. How do we do that?'

'It is almost a day's march, but the route should be safe and unguarded. When you come out of the tunnel you will see the walls of the city behind you. Turn left and follow the line of the city walls for half a mile. Then you will see a gravel road turning to the North West. Follow this road until you reach a row of dead trees on the right hand side. Then head due west – follow the setting sun if you are in doubt – for five miles...' Vishan continued giving his directions. Helen tried to keep up but she had started to lose her concentration. Even the small sip of her drink had made her feel sleepy and unfocused. Luckily Parenon was following every step of the instructions, nodding his understanding as Vishan spoke.

After a couple of minutes Vishan stood and gestured to them to follow him. They walked up to the bar. Ragosh nodded briefly at them and jerked his head to the doorway behind him. They ducked under the bar and made for the door. Parenon looked behind him as they did so. He had been looking all around him while Vishan had been negotiating with Ragosh. He had not seen anything to arouse his suspicions that they were being watched, but as he followed Helen through the door Vishan grabbed his shoulder and pushed him forwards.

'Run my friends! We are betrayed!'

Without hesitation, Parenon scooped Helen up into

his arms and ran down the stone flight of steps on the other side of the door. There was a curtain at the bottom of the stairs. He pushed it aside and leapt through into the darkness. There was the sound of a brief struggle at the top of the stairs behind them. Vishan's voice cried out in sudden pain. Then a door slammed and they heard the clatter of footsteps down the stairs.

Vishan appeared through the curtain. He was clutching at his side. A red stain seeped through his fingers.

'Go, my friends, and hurry!' he winced as he spoke. 'I have dealt with the one who tried to follow us. He paid dearly for attacking me. But others may follow.'

'I am sorry Vishan.' Parenon's voice was desperate; 'I should have kept a closer watch while you were talking with Ragosh. Can I not do anything to help?'

Vishan slumped against the wall. He shook his head. The effort made him wince with pain. 'There is nothing. Go. Quickly.' He sank down onto the floor and his eyes closed. He lay without moving.

There was a banging sound on the closed door above them and angry, shouting voices.

Without looking behind to see what might follow, Parenon and Helen turned and ran into the darkness.

16

A Strange Consultation

When Cleve Harrow walked out of the Great Hall after the meeting with Ungolin and the others, he spent the rest of the afternoon talking with Telenor and those of the Pulver who would accompany him to Atros with Matt and Jenn. He had discussed his plans with them and they all understood the task. It was now the early evening. They had to go soon. But before they could all depart, Cleve Harrow had one more thing that he had to do. There was more information that he wanted.

He made his way down a long dim corridor. It led away from the Pulver's quarters in a room off the Great Hall. From there it wound down many stone steps in a long spiral until it branched out into a network of tunnels which reached far beneath the very foundations of the city. He was going to a place that he did not visit very often. He needed advice. Other people usually came to him with their questions. His opinion was trusted. He would tell them what he thought and other people would usually act on what he, the Cleve, told them. This, however, was very different. Now *he* was the one who needed to ask the questions.

Harrow strode purposefully down tapestry lined corridors. Then his pace began to slow down. Was he right in his decision? The one he was about to consult might not be as helpful as he believed. She had her own view of things. She might not want to help him. Her information might be corrupted by her own desires for a very different outcome. He walked through rooms hung with pictures and with ancient suits of armour decorating the corners. Coats of arms were arrayed along some walls in honour of past generations of the Select, and age-old leaders. Harrow slowed down even more and glanced around him for a moment as he made his way through the rooms. There were other walls almost entirely hidden from view by enormous screens on which a variety of bright, moving images flickered. New technology that provided Ungolin and his followers with a constantly changing scene of information.

Harrow realised that even here, amongst some of the oldest traditions of Beltheron, there was still room for modern invention and innovation. 'The strength of Beltheron,' he considered 'lies in our ability to let the ancient traditions live happily with the new.' He made his way forwards with renewed purpose. 'There is nothing wrong with seeking help from a different quarter. All opinions have a value.' He told himself. 'We cannot be deaf or blind to any information at this time – no matter what its source – be it ancient or modern.'

He took a turning to his left. The corridor was straight and narrow. As he entered the archway that led into the shadows he cast a quick look over his shoulder. There was no one there. He knew that. He was positive that he could not have been followed. Yet he still felt uneasy. He shook his head in irritation at himself. This was not like him. He plunged into the darkness of the corridor.

He walked in near total darkness for three or four minutes. Anyone else would have held their hands in front of them, staggering and stumbling along slowly; but Cleve Harrow knew his way. He strode on.

Eventually he saw a dim, yellowy light up ahead.

Everything around him was silent. The only sounds came from his own footfalls on the stone floor. He drew closer to the light. The corridor opened out onto a wide circular cavern. In the centre was a still pool of water. The yellow light seemed to be coming from under the surface of the water. The light shimmered and threw moving shadows onto the walls and ceiling. A smooth white island rose out of the water in the centre of the pool. The island was only about five metres across. It looked to be made up of a single curved white rock.

A woman stood in the centre of the island. She was clothed in a long, flowing green robe. Her arms hung at her sides and she was perfectly immobile. Her hair was the same yellow colour as the light that came up from the pool, as if it had been dyed by the water. She stared straight ahead of her, not acknowledging that Harrow had entered the cavern. Her eyes were completely white.

'Welcome, friend.' Her voice was low and gentle, with a hint of song in it. 'How can I help you?'

'Greetings, T'yuq Tinyaz.' Harrow bowed down before her. 'I come for advice.'

Her pale eyes shimmered for a brief moment, showing hints of blue and gold, before returning to their blank, impassive white. 'You seek knowledge of the Lady Yelenia.'

Harrow inclined his head to show that this was true.

'I am about to lead a rescue party to Atros to find and rescue her. I wish to know if you can tell me anything that may help me in my quest.'

'Have no fear for that one. She has the power. She is assisted by one who is faithful. He will not let her down. Only death will prevent him from saving her.' T'yuq Tinyaz paused. Her eyes flickered again. 'But there is other danger. The boy.' Harrow stiffened. 'You should not have left him, Cleve. Your student, Orianna Melgardes will try to protect him. It cannot be doubted that she is brave, but some things will rip the courage from even the stoutest of hearts. Go back to them as soon as you can. Do not delay, for evil is in Beltheron and it is not easily vanquished. Go Cleve!' Her voice had risen and although it still kept its song-like quality, now it also held a note of anger. No one who heard it would ever think of arguing with that voice. 'Go! Seek out the boy! You neglect your duty by dallying here.'

Cleve Harrow was already running back towards the darkness of the corridor. He cursed himself under his breath. He should have put a strong guard of Pulver around Jack. It was stupid, *reckless*, not to! If Tur's agents could travel to earth then it was blind madness to suppose that they could not get to Beltheron just as easily. He had to get to them. He had to rescue Jack and Orianna.

17
The Story of Serrion

It had taken Orianna and Jack about fifteen minutes to get back across the crowded city to an area filled with narrow, winding streets. Orianna led the way quickly, occasionally looking over her shoulder. She saw nothing following them that gave her any alarm, but as Jack had so rightly pointed out, the Shifter could look like anything it wanted to by now; they would be none the wiser. Still, nothing had tried to attack or stop them so far and both of them were extremely grateful when they turned away from the bustle of the busy main streets and down quieter alleys. This was clearly one of the older parts of the city, Jack thought. Many of the buildings here had thatched roofs and half timbered walls like the pictures of Tudor homes he had seen in one of his school history books. Finally they reached a long row of terraced cottages. Smoke curled slowly from the chimneys of some, into the early evening sky, and wonderful smells of cooking wafted out as they went past. At last Orianna stopped outside one of the doors and, without pausing to knock, opened the door and stepped inside, telling Jack to follow her.

The inside of the cottage was just about the most comfortable and welcoming that Jack had ever seen. The room that they had walked into directly off the street was obviously the main living area. Dark beams ran across the ceiling, with trailing flowers, beautifully scented, hanging from them. A deep fireplace covered most of one wall. Metal shelves held steaming pots and pans. Jack saw the familiar white-haired figure of Korellia bending over the fire; she stirred the coals with a long metal poker, sending sparks rushing up the chimney and creating a warm rush of air which made Jack's cheeks tingle. She straightened and turned as she heard them enter.

'Orianna, my dear, why and young master Andressen too!'

Orianna walked over to her and kissed her on the forehead. 'Hello Mother,' she said.

Of course! Jack realised; it was obvious that the two were related. One look at their matching white hair would tell anyone that in a moment. If he had not been preoccupied with so many other things in the Great Hall he would have realised.

'Hello Korellia.' He said.

'You have much to thank this young man for;' Orianna told her mother, 'he saved my life this afternoon.'

Korellia's eyes widened in astonishment. 'Oh, tell me, my dears!' She said in a rush. 'Tell me at once what happened!'

As they related their story of the Shifter, Korellia fussed around them, sitting them on a soft couch and going into the next room and back with plates and glasses. By the time that they had reached the part where Jack opened the locked door, both of them already had mouths full of a delicious, rich cake, and glasses of fruity purple juice in their hands.

After they had finished telling their tale, Korellia sat for a few moments in silence. Then, raising herself from the deep thoughts in her head, she looked at the pair of them with affection. A deep love was in her eyes as she gazed at Orianna. Jack felt a stabbing pang in his chest as he realised that his own mother had never looked at him in that way. He felt sure that his mother loved him, but for a moment he felt jealous of the strong feeling which obviously existed between Korellia and her daughter.

His emotion must have been clear on his face. Korellia moved to sit by him. 'Thank you for bringing my daughter safely back to me. I have already lost a son to that evil monster, Gretton Tur. I do not know what I would do if Orianna were to be taken from me as well.' She paused for a moment, thinking about her next words. 'I know that you also have lost loved ones, Jack. But believe me; everything possible is being done by the Council, even as we speak, to try to find a way of reaching them and bringing them back to safety. Tomorrow you must set out with your friends, including my daughter here. Great deeds will be done, and I am sure that you will find those you seek.'

Jack nodded his head slowly, and thanked her for her kind words.

'Korellia?' he began; 'what did happen to your son?'

A cloud passed over Korellia's face, and Orianna reached across to hold her hand tightly. There was sadness in her eyes too.

'He was just a baby;' said Korellia, so quietly that Jack had to lean forwards and listen carefully to make out her words. 'A beautiful little thing.' She looked at Jack. 'How old are you?'

'I'm twelve.'

'Twelve, yes. He would have been about your age, maybe even a little older I suppose. He was born in the winter so he would have been nearly thirteen by now.

'One night, about eleven years ago I was sitting here in front of this very fire with my son, Serrion, on my lap. Orianna was over there, playing on the floor with her doll and some of her toy animals. Her father was at the Great

Hall, he was secretary to the Council at the time and they were meeting late into the night to talk about the opening of the Pathways, and the sightings of the Rish that had been reported in Beltheron. So, there were only the three of us here. Orianna was nine years old, and her hair had just begun to turn white. (It always does in our family you know, sooner or later.) Well, Serrion was just about to fall asleep when there was a bright white light in the sky outside the window. At first we thought that it must be a shooting star, or maybe just the lights of one of those new-fangled machines that everyone loves to fly around on these days. But the light got brighter and brighter until it was really quite dazzling, even though we had the drapes closed, like tonight. Then we both heard the noise. A low humming noise that grew and grew until the walls shook. I will never forget that sound.'

Jack looked at Orianna. Her head was bowed so that her face was hidden by the locks of pure white hair. It was clear that she remembered that long-ago evening as well as her mother.

'I stood to go to the window,' Korellia continued; 'I put Serrion down in his cot by the wall there,' she pointed to a corner of the room, 'and I walked over to pull back the drapes to see what it could be. There was a crash, and the window shattered right in front of me. Long, clawed arms reached through into the room. I turned to run back to my children, to try to protect them, but I was too slow. One of the arms caught at me and pinned me back against the wall. It was the Rish of course. One of them leapt into the room. It was huge, grey, and covered with slime. It crouched for a moment where it had landed then spun around and faced me. I was still held against the wall be the other creature and I thought that I would be killed there and then. The creature just hissed at me, though, and showed rows and rows of black and yellow teeth. Then it turned to Serrion's cot and leapt towards it, reaching in with those abominable limbs. I …I think I screamed for the first time then – for my fear for my children's safety was even greater than that I had for myself.'

Korellia paused again. Now she was staring blankly at the wall where she had described the cot. Jack could tell that she was not really aware of him, Orianna or the room anymore. Her whole imagination was concentrated on that dreadful night of horror, almost twelve years ago.

Still without taking her gaze from the wall, Korellia continued speaking. Her voice was quieter now, but firm and unwavering.

'The Rish picked up little Serrion as if he were just a bundle of rags. I struggled, oh I struggled so hard to try to get free, to help my son, but I could not, I could not. Orianna was so brave. She ran towards the creature. She swung her doll at its legs and struck at it with her fists. It looked down at her and just pushed her away. It did not want her. Only Serrion. Only my son. Just before it leapt out of the room again it hissed into my face again. I could make out the words: 'the mighty Lord, Gretton Tur the Wild, thanks you for the gift of your son.' Then he was gone, and the arm holding me up to the wall released me and coiled back through the window.

'We both ran to the window to look out, but there was another dazzling flash of light. When it faded and our eyes had got used to the darkness again, the Rish and my little Serrion had gone. Friends and neighbours came running, but it was no use. No one could be of any help.' She gave a deep sigh. Jack and Orianna watched her in silence for what seemed like a long time. At last Korellia turned around and looked straight at Jack.

'On that same day Orianna swore to devote herself

to work against the Wild Lord. She became Cleve Harrow's youngest student, and has helped him in his work ever since.'

Korellia finished speaking. The other two remained silent after her story. An air of sadness filled the room. The sun had dropped right down now and no light came in from the window. The fire had burnt down to its embers, leaving a dull orange glow which lit up the three faces and threw dim shadows onto the walls. Jack stared into the embers, thinking about little Serrion. The fire found a final scrap of unspent fuel and with a brief crackle sent one last bright red flare spurting up to the chimney as he watched.

Suddenly Orianna sat up straight. She listened intently, her head slightly tilted towards the door. Then Jack heard it too. A scuffling, sniffing sound just outside. Then there was a loud rap on the door. Korellia got to her feet to answer it, but Orianna shot out her hand to stop her. 'Wait!' she hissed. She and Jack were both on their feet as well by now. Swift as a hawk, Orianna ran silently to the window. She flicked back a corner of the curtain and looked out into the street. Before he knew what he was doing, Jack found himself by the fireplace, picking up the poker that lay at the side of the hearth. Holding it in front of him in both hands, he followed Orianna to the door.

'Who is it?' he mouthed silently to her.

'It looks like the Cleve.' She replied in a low, urgent whisper.

Korellia was beside them now, concern and fear on her face.

'Cleve Harrow?'

Her daughter nodded. 'But I do not think it *is* him. I believe it could be the Shifter.'

'Did you see his face move?' asked Jack.

'No, but it is nearly dark outside. It is very difficult

to recognise a Shifter in the dark. It must have followed us from the square and then waited for darkness just for that reason.'

'Ask him something.' Korellia said, 'You know the Cleve's voice well enough if nothing else.'

Orianna cleared her throat. 'Who is it?'

Silence.

She tried again; 'Harrow, is it you?'

Still nothing.

'That decides it;' Jack said, 'it's *got* to be the Shifter hasn't it? Harrow would have answered us straight away.'

Orianna nodded. 'Quickly! Jack, Mother, out through the back room.'

But as they turned to hurry away from the door there was a mighty thud and a loud crackling sound. Jack spun around, the poker still in his hands, and saw the image of Cleve Harrow bending and buckling the heavy wood of Korellia's front door. Even in the twilight dimness of the room Jack could see that the effort of breaking into the house was too great for the Shifter to keep up his false image at the same time. The face of Harrow flickered and rippled before Jack's eyes, the familiar robes vanished, and for the first time, Jack saw the true form of the Shifter. The sight made him quake with fear. Nothing in his imagination had prepared him for what now stood before him. Once the image of Cleve Harrow had gone, the Shifter grew in size until it was touching the ceiling. Now Jack could see why the creature took on the features of others – because it had no features of its own. The skin of the Shifter looked like muddy water with a thin, oily film covering the whole surface. Its limbs spread out and continuously changed shape, flowing towards Jack. As the limbs got nearer, two pincer shapes sprang from the ends, clacking in front of his face like giant crab's claws.

More in terror than in defiance, Jack swung wildly with the poker. It struck the Shifter in what would have been the centre of its stomach, but instead of hitting flesh, the poker disappeared up to the handle. Still holding on, Jack tried to pull the poker back, so that he could strike again. But the poker was being pulled from his fingers. It was disappearing *into* the Shifter's middle! Jack had to let go before he too was pulled in. He staggered backwards, feeling his way around a chair, never taking his eyes of the nightmare in front of him. He staggered sideways, until he was behind the chair, just as Orianna leapt forwards, swinging a large saucepan at the top half of the Shifter's body. Again it had no effect. The oily skin just swallowed the pan up and carried on moving forwards towards them. Now, to Jack's complete amazement, the Shifter began to create a different shape, with limbs; the poker was reappearing out of the Shifter's new right 'arm'. It waved it angrily, so that it cut viciously through the air, dangerously close to Jack's head. Korellia was already in the other room, opening the back door. Orianna and Jack raced after her, the Shifter close behind them. The poker was now striking madly at everything in its path, knocking things off shelves and scoring deep marks along the walls. It was joined by the pan, which had also reappeared out of another limb. The Shifter flung the pan straight at Orianna. She ducked just in time as the heavy pan smashed into the wall directly behind her.

The back door was now open and the three of them raced through. Jack was the last to go through and just as the door was about to slam closed behind him the Shifter lunged into the frame. Limbs snaked out and grabbed Jack by the throat. He choked as he staggered back towards the glistening monster. Its touch was freezing cold and he felt his neck and shoulder go numb where it held him.

Dizziness swept over him. The last thing that Jack was aware of was Orianna's voice screaming, and the sight of four other creatures with egg-shaped heads and slits for eyes, waiting for them in the alleyway behind Korellia's house. 'The Rish! The Rish are here,' he thought, as darkness closed around him.

When Cleve Harrow arrived at the house in a blinding flash of light just a few minutes later, the house was in darkness. He was too late. Jack, Orianna and Korellia were now the hostages of the enemy.

18
The Captives

Gendrell, (or Atros City as it was first called,) was as dark, ugly and uninviting as Beltheron's Capital City was colourful, exciting and welcoming. The buildings of Gendrell were all constructed from the same black stone. There was none of Beltheron's beauty. Beltheron had a variety of structures designed and built over the centuries by many talented and visionary architects and artists, but Gendrell was the work of just one man: Gretton Tur the Wild Lord. He delighted in the dark stone, the threatening walls and the corridors, which led to torture chambers, dungeons, and underground lairs for his morbid creations. These dank tunnels went as far underground as the forbidding towers rose above it. It was here, deep in the mud and stink and slime that Gretton Tur worked his magic, and practised his evil skills. Throughout the damp and stinking passageways he went, revelling in his growing power, and thinking only of the time, soon now, oh very soon, when his plans would all ripen; when his victory in *all* the worlds would be assured. His Rish would soon travel freely to Beltheron and to Earth itself, without this ridiculous need for secrecy. Soon there would be nothing to stop them preparing for his glorious return. His success would be complete, his triumph total. That fool Harrow thought that he could force the mighty Gretton Tur to his knees by bringing together two ridiculous children out of an old fairy tale! Well he knew better! Those children could not help Beltheron's plight. Gretton Tur was ahead of them all. They would never know the true cunning of his plans until it was too late. One of those children whom Cleve Harrow held so dear was now Gretton Tur's prisoner, down in his deepest dungeon. How easy it had been. Soon the other child would also be in his clutches, and the proud prophesy of the ludicrous Council would turn to ashes. The so called Wise Council of Beltheron would have the deaths of two children on their consciences. He, Gretton Tur was in charge now. Soon he would control the Golden Staff and soon, all would tremble before him.

He came at last to the bars of the dungeon where Jack, Orianna and Korellia were being held captive. They had been carried down into the depths and thrown into the cell by the same four Rish who had captured them outside Korellia's house. Jack was still unconscious after his battle with the Shifter; he knew nothing of their journey with the Rish along the Pathway. He now lay on the floor of the cell with his head cradled in Orianna's lap.

Korellia was crouching in a far corner. She looked completely distraught, and all she could do was to keep repeating to herself; '*again* – they came back *again*,' over and over to herself.

Gretton Tur reached the door and gazed down at the scene. Orianna felt a cold breeze blow across her face as he looked at her. She turned to stare back at the Wild Lord. In his hand he held a long, carved staff. It was very similar to the Golden Staff of Beltheron, but this one was completely black. The carvings on it made her shudder. Tur's eyes showed a strange mixture of contempt and cold amusement as he glared at Orianna.

'So, Dove-hair, at last you have come to visit me. I

am absolutely delighted.' His cold gaze passed briefly over Korellia and Jack. He grinned wickedly. 'I see you have brought the old crone and the innocent with you. No doubt you are pleased that you can now have a family reunion?'

Orianna's eyes suddenly grew wide, and she spoke at last. 'A reunion? Family reunion? Do you mean that my Brother is here? I must see him. I demand you take me to my brother. Where is he?'

Gretton Tur cackled. 'You will see. Soon, soon. I promise you will see. And then you will understand. But now, forgive me, Dove-hair. I must leave you. I wanted to see the innocent boy that you all expect so much of. It amuses me. But other things forever press my time. Farewell for now.'

Tur's laughter grew louder as he turned, and then echoed around the cold walls as he left them. Orianna shivered again, and then, as The Wild Lord retreated, the air seemed to grow a little warmer. Jack moaned and sat up.

'Orianna? Where are we?'

'On Atros, my dear.'

The information reached him slowly. Painfully. His head throbbed steadily. Each pounding in his temples felt like a knife being twisted in his skull. Jack reached up to rub his forehead, to try to relieve some of the agony. He felt dampness under his hand. Drawing it away he looked down and saw deep reddish brown stains on the tips of his fingers.

'Here.' Orianna lifted a corner of her torn sleeve and wiped some of the blood from his face. 'You struck your head when you fell, battling with the Shifter. You will be all right. I do not think the wound is a deep one.'

'The Shifter? Oh yes. Of course; I remember. And the Rish? They were there too?'

Orianna nodded. 'Yes. The Shifter must have led them to the house. They waited outside until darkness and then they attacked. There was nothing we could do against such might. But you showed tremendous bravery Jack. Mother and I are both very grateful.'

Jack turned around to look at Korellia. She was still rocking gently back and forth, murmuring to herself. 'My poor little Serrion, is this where they brought you, all those years ago?'

Jack got up and walked to the heavy metal bars of the cell. The door was locked and bolted securely. Wrapped around the bars of the door there was a rusty chain with another large padlock holding it securely in place.

Jack glanced back at Orianna. She was looking at him carefully. Then she got to her feet and joined him by the cell door. They both looked down at the locks and chains.

'Are you thinking what I am, Orianna?'

'Do you think you can do it?

'I won't know if I don't try, will I?'

'Wait!' Orianna gripped the bars and held her face towards the gloom of the passageway. Her eyes narrowed as she peered into the darkness. She listened intently for a moment. Then she called out down the corridor where Gretton Tur had walked a minute before.

'Hey there! You miserable beasts! You can't just leave us all down here. Come back!'

They both listened intently. There was no reply. She called out again.

'I said come back here. There's something I want to tell you all. It's important.'

They waited. There was still no reply. No returning footsteps. No one who was curious to hear what Orianna might have to say.

She looked down at Jack again.

'It looks as if we're alone.' He said to her. 'I think that they've gone.'

Orianna nodded. 'I think you're right. Try the door Jack. Try it now.'

Jack raised his hands towards the chain and the padlock first. He felt the tingling starting in his fingers. The sensation was beginning to be familiar to him now. Holding his hands just above the lock they both gasped as the chains twitched. There was a rusty scraping sound and the padlock sprang open.

'Well done, Jack!' Orianna took the padlock from the chain and started to unwind it from around the bars of the door. At the same time Jack had started to work on the lock of the door itself. Holding his hands centimetres from the large keyhole he waited for the tingling in his fingers. Nothing happened for a few seconds. He closed his eyes and concentrated. His fingers were stretched out, tense and rigid. The image of the golden staff came into his mind, the way he had seen it for the first time when the cords of Cleve Harrow's black bag had opened up. As this image came into his mind there was a creaking sound and the door swung slowly open.

He breathed a sigh of relief. Orianna clutched his shoulder tightly.

'Thank you Jack. Well done.'

He felt a glow in his stomach again, happy that he had been some use to them once more. His feeling of pride filled him with more courage than he had felt since this whole incredible adventure had begun. He looked up into Orianna's face.

'Come on.' He said. 'I'm going to get us out of here.'

19
The Pedjiaar Trap

Parenon stopped at the top of the hill and looked all around him. After their escape from Atros City they had travelled until nightfall and then hidden and rested. It had taken them most of the next day to reach this high look-out point. Vishan had given them clear directions and his descriptions of landmarks to watch for along the way had been precise. But even so the route had been a long one and the late afternoon sun was sinking behind the distant trees ahead of them in the west. Parenon and Helen both had to screw up their eyes to see properly. Down the other side of the hill more trees could be seen stretching away into a large wood. It looked dark in there and a little bit forbidding, but it was down there that Parenon was directing most of his attention.

'That looks like the wood that Vishan told us to look out for. But even without his advice I would have said that it was a good place for a group of rebels to hide out.'

'What makes you say that, Parenon?'

'There are no clear ways into the forest without being seen from a long way off. The only track leading into the woods is this one, and it is clearly visible to anyone who is sitting in any of those high branches.' He pointed to a strand of trees growing taller than most of the others, about a hundred metres into the wood. They did indeed look like ideal lookout posts.

'The forest looks thick and overgrown.' Parenon went on. 'If you did make this place your hideaway, any strangers trying to find you in there would be at a great disadvantage. If you had any knowledge of the place at all it would be easy to lose any of your pursuers. They could wander about for days without finding a way out.'

'Are you sure that we should be going in there then?' Helen sounded worried.

'I think we must.' He smiled down at her. 'Do not worry too much about what I have just said. We will not get lost. Remember I have many skills in tracking and forest lore. We are as safe inside that forest as anywhere else.

'But how do you know that we won't be seen?'

'I do not know. But I have been looking at those trees very carefully now for several minutes. I have seen no movement, and, as you know my eyes are keen and strong. I do not think that anyone is on the look out at the moment.'

There was silence between the two of them for a moment. Then Parenon cleared his throat and spoke in a low voice. 'I… I think that it is safe for us to seek these people, these rebels, but I cannot be sure.' He turned quickly to face her. His face was so serious that Helen had difficulty holding his gaze.

'Vishan was sure.' She said. She felt embarrassed for a moment at mentioning Vishan's name. She knew that Parenon considered himself at fault for not noticing the person in the bar who had killed Vishan.

Parenon was staring down at the ground. His face was in torment.

'Helen, do you…do you trust me?'

She nodded her head vehemently. 'Yes Parenon, of course I do! You mustn't blame yourself for what went wrong earlier.'

'Thank you.'

'We're in this together Parenon. It is not your fault that Vishan was killed. And if it hadn't been for you, the Rish would have captured me straight away. I know that you will do your best to protect me. I trust you with my life, and I know that my trust is not misplaced.' She took his hand in both of her own and squeezed tightly.

As they made their way through the trees the ground began to level out. There was a little clearing just up ahead of them. No trees grew here. Helen looked straight up into the sky and saw some dark clouds passing slowly across the late afternoon sky. It grew suddenly darker and she shivered. The air was getting chilly. Parenon was a few steps ahead of her, and on her right hand side. He was looking closely at the ground. He stopped moving forwards and shot his hand out in a warning.

'Tread carefully, Helen.' He warned. 'Be as silent as you can. I don't like the feel of this pl.. .'

Even as he was speaking, Helen stepped on a particularly loud twig. As it snapped under her feet she felt the ground tilting away. There was more snapping and crackling and Parenon hurled himself towards her.

'Jump!' he cried. But it was too late. Even as his hand reached her shoulder to push her out of the way of the trap that had been laid in the floor of the clearing, the rest of the twigs and branches disappeared under their feet and both of them tumbled into a broad pit.

Somehow, Parenon had managed to get his arms around Helen's waist and turn himself in the air so that he was underneath her. In this way he cushioned her fall when they landed. Even so, she felt winded, and she heard Parenon's own gasp of pain with a guilty feeling. She rolled off him quickly.

'Are you all right?' he grunted.

'I think so. Thanks for catching me.'

Parenon was already halfway onto his feet. He looked up. The pit was at least three metres deep. It was obvious that, tall as he was, even he could not reach the top. The walls of the pit were almost vertical. He placed his hand on them. They were very smooth. There were no hand or footholds anywhere to be seen. Not only that, but the orangey brown earth was wet and clay-like. Helen put her own hand against it and felt how slippery it was. Parenon's face furrowed into worried lines for a moment. Then he dropped into a crouch and sprang into the air. Helen had never seen anyone spring so high like that from a standing position. But it was not enough. He tried to get hold of some roots or embedded stones at the rim of the pit with his fingers but it was useless. He slithered back into the trap immediately. A few more clods of slippery orange clay came away from the wall.

'Once again I fail today.' He murmured grimly. 'But I do not give up easily.' He reached to his side and drew his long sword. 'This may not be of as much use to us here as a spade or a pickaxe would be,' he grinned. 'But it may suffice.'

As Helen watched he began to stab at the clay. Large chunks of it came away from the wall at once. He sliced and cut with the sharp blade. After just a minute or so, Parenon had succeeded in creating a crudely shaped step in the side of the pit. He had made it so that it dipped down inside, away from the outer edge, to give them something to hold onto as they climbed up.

'That will work!' Helen shouted excitedly. 'We will soon be able to climb out at this rate. What can I do to help?' In spite of all that had happened to them, she instinctively felt optimistic about their plight. She thought it impossible that her brave companion and protector would not be able to get them safely out of any fix.

Parenon had not stopped his digging. 'Clear away some of this pile of filth that is gathering around my feet. Already it is clogging up my way and making it difficult for me to dig effectively.'

Helen dropped to her knees, wincing as she did so. For the moment in all the excitement, she had forgotten about her wounds. It did not stop her work though. She and Parenon continued to work furiously to dig their way up and out of their trap.

'Who do you think dug this in the first place?' she asked him.

'Undoubtedly the rebels we are seeking. Whether to catch the Rish and other enemies, or just to trap food I cannot say.'

'But if you think that they are on our side, then surely we don't have anything to fear from them. We could just wait until they…'

'I am afraid not.' Parenon had finally stopped his urgent digging and turned to look at her. 'I dare not just sit here and wait. It is true that the people who dig this trap might not intend us any harm. But we are in a desperate situation nevertheless. Here in this pit I can hardly swing my sword enough to dig our way out. I certainly could not fight down here. And there are other creatures who may wander this forest apart from the rebels; I have no doubt about that. What if the Rish were to discover us first? No Helen, we must get out. As long as we are in this trap we are a … a…. a lying goose!'

'A what, Parenon?'

'It is a saying that I have heard your mother and father use. A lying goose. You must have heard it. It means we are an easy target, we are..'

Helen burst out laughing. 'Oh Parenon! It's not a lying goose, silly! It's a sitting duck!'

She continued to laugh at his mistake. But Parenon was not laughing. He wasn't even looking at her. His eyes were fixed at a point above and behind her head. Helen's own laugh died in her throat. He was very still, even his eyes did not move from whatever he was staring at.

'What is it?' she asked, and began to turn around.

'Quiet and be very still!' His whispered words were spat out rapidly between clenched teeth. 'It may not see us if we stay still and silent.'

Helen did as she was told. She stood as still as she possible could, gazing up at Parenon's fixed expression, as he in turn glared at whatever it was behind her at the top of the pit.

Then she heard the growl. In spite of Parenon's warning, Helen turned around very slowly and raised her eyes.

Above them was a tiger-like creature. That is to say, it was the same size and shape as a regular tiger. It even had stripes, but these stripes were red and grey, not orange and black. The teeth in the animal's wide jaws were serrated, like those of a shark. It was staring with deep, crimson eyes directly at Helen. It licked its lips. She shuddered in terror.

'Do not move, I said!' Parenon repeated in a low hiss. 'It is a pedjiaar. They sense movement. But otherwise their eyes are poor'

Helen thought for a moment about the birds in her garden at home and how her father had told her that if she stayed still they would not notice that she was there and she would be able to watch them. But it was hard not to shake, or whimper aloud when such a fearsome creature appeared to have her on the menu.

They stood stock still for what seemed like an age. The pedjiaar sniffed a couple of times. It dropped its head lower into the pit. Helen felt sure that it must know that they were there. Then a low growl came up from deep in its throat. The pedjiaar began to salivate and drops of greasy fluid dripped from its jaws and down towards them. The huge paws of the hunter flexed at the edge of the pit and it looked as if it was ready to jump. Helen tensed up even more and she felt even Parenon brace himself next to her, moving his hand slightly to the hilt of his sword.

Suddenly another sound broke from the forest trees beyond their line of vision. It sounded like the crashing of many hurried footsteps over broken twigs and dry leaves. The pedjiaar lifted its head and turned swiftly to face the direction of this new noise. The low growl grew louder into a mighty roar and it sprang away from the top of the pit. Human voices were now heard, yelling defiance at the creature. Helen and Parenon could see nothing of what was happening above them from their refuge in the bottom of the trap, but Helen imagined it must be a fearful battle. Jeering shouts and cries mingled with louder and angrier roars and growls. Once or twice Helen heard a snapping, cracking sound like a whip and the low dull thud as of heavy foot – or paw – steps on the ground. The scuffling continued for several seconds more, and then there was an anguished yelp from the Pedjiaar the sound of the heavy paws scurrying away, and finally a cheering from the human voices.

'That is a hopeful sound' Parenon muttered. 'Let us hope that whoever has defeated the creature will be friendly towards us.'

No sooner had he said these words than another head peered over the edge of the pit. It was a man, not very old, Helen thought to herself, probably no more than seventeen or eighteen years. His blond hair was cropped short and he had an inquisitive, amused expression on his face.

'Good day to you.' He said. 'You are not quite what we hoped to catch for dinner this evening, but if we can't eat you, I suppose the least we can do is invite you to join us...' he broke off to laugh briefly, '...*at* the table instead of *on* it!'

'Your hospitality is most welcome and we accept it with thanks.' Parenon replied. 'It would be more welcome however if it was accompanied by a ladder, or some other means of getting out of this pit.'

The young man laughed again. 'Without further ado! Marel, Sherin, some ropes here!'

Coils of thin woven strands tumbled down towards them, and with Parenon's help Helen was able to scramble up towards the helping hands reaching from above.

They were soon out of the pit, standing in the middle of a group of about a dozen men and women. They all wore dark leather clothing and had bows and quivers full of arrows slung at their backs. Some had cloaks over their shoulders which fell all the way to the ground. They were of different ages, from teenagers like the young man they had first seen, ranging all the way to a couple of more elderly figures that Helen guessed were in their late fifties or sixties. All of them wore their hair cropped close to their skulls and all looked as if they were extremely physically fit, slim but muscled and quick moving.

The young man spoke. 'Welcome to our forest. I am Tarawen, leader of the rebels against Gretton Tur.'

'We are grateful to you for your help.' Parenon replied. 'However, I am surprised that you should give us your identities so easily. If you are indeed the rebels who fight against The Wild Lord, how do you know that you can trust us with that knowledge?'

'My agents are extremely skilled in shadowing and

following trails,' said Tarawen. 'Sherin here was following you and listening to your conversations for some time. He heard more than enough to convince him that you would be sympathetic, and possibly even useful to our cause. Unfortunately, when he left you to come to find me and tell me of your approach, you fell into one of our many traps. We were on our way to intercept you and welcome you to our camp when we heard the noises of the pedjiaar and guessed the outcome of your wandering.'

'Then we are both most grateful for your assistance and offer of friendship.' Parenon put out his hand and Tarawen grasped it warmly.

'Come, we mentioned food, and you look as if you would benefit from a decent meal.'

During this conversation, Helen noticed that one of the older women gathered around them had begun to stare at her with interest. The woman reached into her leather tunic and brought out a silver chain with something attached to it. It was about the size of a large coin, but was square in shape instead of round. The woman gazed at it for a moment. She looked up at Helen again and then back at the coin, before her face broke into an excited grin.

'It is her!' She said breathlessly. It is the Lady Yelenia. She has come among us!'

Everyone turned back to Helen. The woman was holding out the coin for them to see. Parenon stepped up to her and took the coin in his fingers. He looked down at the image carved there. It was indeed Helen. Parenon turned the coin over. On the other side was a perfectly recognisable interpretation of Jack's face. Tarawen was now at his side.

'Well, if we had needed any further proof of your friendship, here it is. This is well met indeed.' He turned to Helen and dropped down onto one knee. His hand reached into his belt and he drew a long knife from its sheath. Holding it out towards her with both hands, he lowered his head. All of his companions were kneeling now and looking down towards the ground. Helen felt the blood rushing to her cheeks. This was embarrassing. Had she known it, Jack had felt exactly the same thing when he realised that everyone in the Great Hall in Beltheron was bowing down to him. Unlike Jack of course, Helen was used to the knowledge that she was Select. She had already experienced several occasions when people had bowed down to her, showing their reverence. She still felt uncomfortable when it happened though, and unworthy of such attention.

One of the rebels rose to his feet. 'We are honoured indeed, Lady Yelenia. All our legends tell that you have a place in our struggle, a noble part to play.'

'That's what they all say.' She thought to herself. 'I just wish I knew what it was.'

20

Escape into the Tunnel

Everything was dark in the tunnel ahead of them. The only light came from a torch on one of the walls. Jack reached up and took it down from its sconce.

'I think that we'll need this.'

Orianna nodded. She and Korellia stood side by side looking down at him. Jack realised that they were waiting for him to make a decision. He looked up and down the corridor.

'We need to move quickly.' He said. 'The Rish or something even worse, could be back any minute.'

'None of us have any idea of which way to go.' Orianna said. 'I think that the best thing is to go in the same direction that Gretton Tur went when he left us in the cell.'

'I agree.' Jack said after a moment's thought. 'For some reason – and I can't explain it at all – but I think that we're deep underground. Tur was probably on his way to the surface.

'The air is certainly stale enough for this to be an underground system of caves. And it feels heavy somehow, as if there were a great weight of rock and stone over our heads.' Jack sighed, 'although I doubt that makes any sense.'

Orianna shook her head. 'Nothing makes sense in this place.'

Korellia spoke for the first time. 'We could follow the Wild Lord,' she said, 'but my instinct tells me to get as far away from him as we can. I just want to run in the opposite direction. He may have been on his way to the surface. But he might just as easily have been going to taunt other poor prisoners.' She peered at both of them in the guttering light of the torch. 'What would the purpose be in following him only to reach another cell?'

It seemed an impossible decision. Either choice could lead equally to escape or to disaster. Eventually it was Jack who spoke.

'We have to do something at any rate. The only certain thing is that if we just stand here we will never get out. I think that we should go that way.' He pointed in the opposite direction to where Gretton Tur had gone. 'If we do then at least we know that we are getting further from the Wild Lord. If we don't find any other corridors leading up, or if things feel really bad down there, we can always come back this way.'

Orianna agreed. 'I do not feel keen to follow Tur either.' She said. 'Let us take careful note of our steps so that we can find our way back if need be. For whatever route we take I fear that it will be a long one.'

'Come then.' Korellia said decisively. 'Let us start. Jacques, my dear, would you be so good as to lead the way with your torch?'

They set off down the dark passageway. Looming shadows appeared on every side from the flickering torch in Jack's hand. Every few minutes one of the shadows would seem to be a little deeper and darker. When this happened they would pause to peer into the small caves and crevices at the sides of the corridor to see if it was another opening onto a different path. But each time they looked it was just a recess made by an ancient rock fall, or some old digging work that had been abandoned almost as soon as it had begun. Jack shivered inside as he wondered about the hands that had done the digging.

They staggered on for what seemed like another half an hour. There had been no other passage or turning in the corridor to left or right. It did not rise up or drop down. It just seemed to go on and on.

The torch in Jack's hand was getting dimmer. It was getting more and more difficult to see ahead. The thought of the torch going out altogether and leaving them in total blackness terrified him. He slowed his pace. Orianna put her hand on his shoulder.

'Can you see something Jack?'

He peered into the gloom in front of them. 'No. Nothing. I think we made a mistake coming this way. We must have walked more than a mile. I don't think we should go any further. Our light won't last much longer. If we hurry, and make our way back to the dungeons, at least we might be able to find more torches.'

'I agree with you.' Orianna said.

'But our escape might have been discovered by now.' Korellia added. 'They might be looking for us.'

Jack pondered this for a moment. He could not stop thinking about the darkness when the torch finally burnt out. He glanced at it again. It seemed to be getting dimmer every minute. But the idea that they might turn back now towards certain capture when they might be very close to a way of escape was almost too much for him to bear. He stood as if rooted to the spot with indecision.

Orianna seemed to be thinking the same thing. 'I think we should continue for five more minutes.' She said. 'We may be just a few paces from a doorway, or a bend in the passage that shows us some light up ahead. I think we should go on. I can't stand to turn back to *Him*, whatever the cost.'

It was decided. They set off along the passageway, huddled together for comfort. But what real comfort could there be, if they did not discover a way out soon, or if the torch burnt out?

However, they had not been going very long this time, when Jack stopped and stiffened. Orianna was so close behind him that she bumped into his back.

"What is it?"

"I think there's another doorway." He held up the torch to show the side of the passageway. "It looks different to the others and it goes further back."

Orianna looked closely. "You're right." She held up her hand towards the door handle.

"Be careful my dear." Korellia warned from behind them. "We are still a long way from safety.

Orianna's hand was already on the door. She pushed the handle down and to her surprise the door began to creak open.

"It worked!" she cried. "Maybe this *is* a way out!"

"We have to try it anyway," Jack continued. "Any chance is better than... phew! What a terrible stink!"

Orianna's nose also wrinkled in disgust. Whatever was in the room or corridor behind the door did smell horrible, as if some terrible creature had died in there and had been rotting away for years. Korellia backed away from the door.

"I don't like this." She said to the others. I don't think that we should..."

It was too late. Both Jack and Orianna had felt so relieved to finally find a doorway that opened, that their sense of relief was much stronger than their sense of possible danger. They had already pushed the door wider and were disappearing into the recesses within. Korellia had no choice. She did not want to be left behind. She plunged into the darkness after them.

If the three companions had known a little more about the history of the caves they would not have been so hasty. The blood bats of Atros had kept their homes in the caverns below the city for many years. Long before the Wild Lord had set up his domain in the fortresses above they had dwelt in the deep shadows, flying out at night through unknown routes to hunt and feed. Long before his arrival in that land, for uncountable years before he had created the Rish, the bats had lived on grubs and small reptiles that scratched away on the surface. In more recent times, they had discovered the taste of Rish meat, and – to them – it was good.

Gretton Tur had known of the bats for a long time. It was he who had placed the door there to block their direct access to his tunnels and castle. He often used the bats as a terrifying threat to ensure loyal service from his minions. He also enjoyed watching his prisoners plead for mercy in front of that door before being flung into the darkness to meet their fate. If Jack and Orianna had known of the blood bats, they would never have opened the ancient door. But stories of the bats had not reached Beltheron. They had never been written about in any of the books which Orianna had studied with Cleve Harrow. Even he did not know of their existence. No one outside of Atros did. No one could, for no one had ever come back through that door to tell what lay beyond...

Jack led the way with Orianna and Korellia close at his heels. This new passage was already looking hopeful. It was beginning to climb gradually, and even though the stench was still horribly strong, there was a sense of fresher, cooler air blowing onto their faces as well.

Jack's heart was beating faster, partly because of the rapid pace they were making up the slope, but more through excitement that it looked as if he was leading them to safety.

'I think we were right to come this way.'

'It does feel more hopeful.'

'The air is a bit better here anyway.'

Korellia was still not convinced. She brought up the rear and did not join in with the conversation. Instead she listened carefully. There was something not quite right about this. She looked up at the rough ceiling above them. It was filled with cracks and shadows. Suddenly she thought she saw a movement. Don't be ridiculous, she told herself. Rock doesn't move. She shook her head and hurried to keep up. Foolish old woman, your mind is playing tricks. Even so she could not resist looking up once more. As she raised her eyes there it was again! A quick, jerky movement. She hadn't imagined it! It appeared yet again, and there was another further along in front of them. This time there was not just a movement, but several bright, glittering pinpoints of yellow light. As she looked, they seemed to flicker on and off. And then she realised what they were, eyes!

Korellia opened her mouth to cry out a warning but before she could utter a sound the air around them erupted in a flurry of leathery wings.

21
Tur's Final Plan

'Get in here now Crudpile, before I blast your worthless hide into the oblivion that it deserves!'

Gretton Tur's voice rasped out like old rusty metal being twisted apart. The venom, anger and hatred in the words made Crudpile cringe into the shadows of the hallway in terror. He shook uncontrollably. How could his plan have gone so wrong? He was supposed to have been the hero, bringing two important prisoners and useful news to the Wild Lord, who would then have been so grateful that he would have lavished reward and riches onto his deserving shoulders. Instead here he was, cowering in a corner, about to be punished in numerous, horrific ways that he did not even dare think about. Curse that Parenon fellow and the young girl for making him look such a fool.

'I said NOW! You snivelling idiot! Do you dare to defy me?'

'N...no master! I am here your Lordship, just on my way.'

Spurred on by sheer terror at the thought that his punishment would be made even worse if he delayed any longer, Crudpile scurried from his dim corner of the corridor and through the open door into Gretton Tur's Chamber.

There sat The Wild Lord, on a wide, black throne. The

arms of the throne spread outwards into long tentacles, each with a claw at the end. Behind Gretton Tur's head, the back of the chair ascended high up towards the ceiling, splitting into razor sharp spikes on which were hung skulls and decaying heads of many sizes and shapes. As Crudpile looked up at them, he realised in horror that he was probably only a couple of ill-chosen replies away from joining them. He must not anger the Wild Lord any more than he had already. Even in his fear, he was turning over ideas and excuses in his mind. Perhaps he could still bring this desperate situation to his advantage.

'Word has come to me that you know of two trespassers in my land.' Tur's voice had sunk to a lower murmur, but it still held Crudpile in its thrall. He could not find the breath to answer.

'Is this true? Do you know of the presence of traitors in Atros City?'

'Yes, L…Lord.'

'And was it you who helped them to get into the city?'

Crudpile suddenly found his voice again and blurted out all at once: 'They tricked me my Lord. I meant to trap them, to bring them to you as a prize, for your own glory and honour my Lord.'

'That would have been praiseworthy. That is what I would have wanted you to do.'

Crudpile felt the first glimmer of hopeful relief. He burbled on again, his words tripping over themselves in haste as he tried to make the most of the slim advantage that he felt he might have with Tur. 'But they were wily and sly, Master. They are evil and, I will admit it, too clever for me. The man Parenon was a Pulver, and I have no power over such as him. But I can still help you, gracious Lord. I can tell you where they are – or at least where I think they are heading.'

Tur's glare softened for a moment and he leaned forward on his dark throne.

'Yes. Tell me.' His mouth twisted into a terrifying smile. 'Tell me now where they are going.'

'The last time that Dross and I were out scaveng... searching for things to sell in the market place, we stumbled on a group of rebels living in the woods.'

'Rebels?'

'Yes, Lord. I can tell you exactly where they are. I can even take the Rish to them, so that the wicked villains can be captured and brought here to your dungeons.'

'That is all to the good. But what have the Rebels got to do with Parenon and the girl?'

'We mentioned the Rebels to them, my Lord. The man Parenon was very interested. It was clear that he meant to join the Rebels, or at least go to them to ask for aid and shelter.'

Gretton Tur was silent. His eyes gazed at the ground as he considered what he was going to do next. The silence stretched out for over a minute until, at last, his cruel mouth slowly curled into a grin. He rose out of his throne and stepped down of the dais. He stood in front of Crudpile's cowering body, bending down until his head was only centimetres from the terrified man's face.

'Tell me, Crudpile; are you courageous or cowardly?'

'I... I will try to be courageous in your service, Master.'

'A wise answer. You will *need* courage for what I have in mind.'

Crudpile gulped. His hope of a minute ago faded. This was getting worse and worse.

'You will help me. You will prove that you are not a worthless fool. I must have that wretch of a Select, the girl Yelenia. And the Pulver trash, that Parenon, he has troubled me for longer than enough. You will make sure that the Pulver is killed and that the Select is brought here to me. Ride out with the Rish. Show them the rebel camp.' Gretton Tur's voice lowered to a smiling whisper. His words now came out more slowly. 'But another will go with you as well. One from whom there will be no escape. One from whom even the Rish cower in awe and terror. Oh, believe me; you will need all your courage to ride with that one.' Tur straightened and raised his voice once more to its original grating rasp. 'Go! Go now! Guide them to the Rebels. They will do the rest.'

'Yes, Master, I will do it, I will do whatever you say!'

Crudpile staggered backwards as he spoke, turning to flee from the presence of the Wild Lord. As he ran the voice of Gretton Tur rose into a wild maniacal laughter which rang around the dark shadows and echoed in the deep, damp recesses of the hall.

22
In the Rebel camp

The group of rebels were making Helen and Parenon feel quite at home. One of the women had taken Helen to the tents at the far side of the camp and fitted her with a green tunic and leggings similar to those worn by the other rebels. At last she was able to get rid of the flappy dressing gown and pyjamas. They also found her a stout pair of leather shoes to replace her slippers. One of the women inspected her injured ankle and bound it tightly with bandages and cords. She had soaked the bandage in a musty smelling liquid before wrapping it around Helen's leg and it made her nose wrinkle in distaste. However, she found that her foot stopped hurting almost immediately, and so she felt that she could put up with the smell.

After thanking the women, Helen made her way back to the campfire. Parenon and Tarawen were deep in conversation. There were delicious aromas swirling around the fire and Helen's stomach gave a loud rumble. In all the excitement she had almost forgotten that they had not eaten all day.

She settled down at the fireside next to Parenon.

Sherin handed her a wooden plate which was piled high with vegetables and strips of pale meat. There was a rich, red sauce covering most of the plate and Helen tucked in greedily.

'Mmm! It's delicious!' she grinned at Tarawen.

'Eat up, there's plenty more.'

Helen had soon finished her first plateful and held it out gratefully for a second helping. The meat was quite chewy, but it had a strong, tangy flavour that she liked.

'This is really tasty,' she said as she filled her mouth with another strip of the meat. 'What is it?'

'It is a great delicacy amongst the rebels, Lady Yelenia.' Tarawen answered. 'And there is plenty of it at the moment after our last raid.'

'Raid?' Helen replied with her mouth full.

'That's right, we captured it a week ago, the last time we attacked the Rish. It is holva meat.'

'Helen stopped chewing. She lowered the fork to her plate and put it down. She had been eating holva? She shuddered. Parenon smiled affectionately at her.

'Don't worry too much.' He laughed. 'It didn't seem so bad until you knew what it was!'

'Yes, but…eugh!'

Tarawen leant forward with another ladle full of the meat and sauce.

'Another helping, Lady?'

Now everyone around the campfire was laughing. At last, Helen joined in.

'Thanks – but no thanks, Tarawen. I think I'm quite full this time.'

She grinned around at them all but as her gaze fell upon Parenon's face, her smile faded. All traces of laughter had gone from his expression; he was staring intently at the trees just beyond the clearing, just as he had when he had seen the pedjiaar. Sherin had also turned to look in the same direction. He held his hand up to silence the rest of them. Parenon leapt quickly and silently to his feet.

Helen whispered breathlessly. 'What is it Parenon?'

'I'm not sure. There was a movement in the bushes.' He looked again. 'There! Beyond the first trees.' He gestured with his arm. Sherin was looking anxiously from one side to the other. Tarawen began walking slowly towards the edge of the trees where Parenon had indicated.

They heard a sudden, throbbing sound coming from the undergrowth. Tarawen froze in his tracks. Helen stiffened. 'What now?' she thought to herself. A gust of hot air blew onto her face from the trees.

The leaves rustled once more, stirred up into swirling eddies by the disturbance in the air. Sherin and Parenon both drew their swords. Instinctively Parenon grabbed Helen and moved her behind him. The throbbing sound increased.

'A Pathway.' Helen whispered to herself as she recognised the sounds.

'When I tell you, run for the trees.' Sherin said. 'Both of you.'

Parenon opened his mouth to reply but Sherin stopped him with a sharp gesture with his hand. "I know your bravery and ability in a fight, but the Lady Yelenia needs you to guard her. I will hold whatever this thing is until you can get away.'

The column of light was clear now, a bright shining white in the air. The Pathway would open in a matter of seconds. 'Run, go now!' Sherin yelled. Parenon knew it was useless to argue and that Sherin was right. He turned and pushed Helen in front of him as they both started to run. There was a blinding flash behind them and at the same instant the throbbing sound stopped. 'Faster Helen, as fast as you can!' Parenon yelled.

'Gracious me, what sort of a welcome is this for a weary traveller?' called out an oddly familiar voice behind them. Parenon slowed down and turned. Sherin had lowered his sword. Standing in front of him, with the Golden Staff in his hands and an amused smile on his face was Cleve Harrow!

They all cried out in surprise and joy at the sight of him.

Helen ran forwards and hugged him. He had been a regular visitor to her house on earth, but she had not seen him recently. His appearance at this moment was more than welcome. Harrow ruffled her hair affectionately as Parenon stepped up to him and bowed.

'Good to see you both safe, Parenon.'

'And you too, sir.'

Helen looked up at him. She still had a big grin on her face. He smiled back.

'You led me quite a chase between the two of you.' He said with a twinkle in his eye.

'But how did you know where to find us?' Helen asked the Cleve. 'How did you create a pathway in the right place? We thought that no one could do that. Apart from me of course. We thought that no one would be able to find us here.'

'She is right.' Parenon went on. 'How in the three worlds did you know where to find us, Cleve?'

They heard someone clear his throat behind them. 'That would be me.' Everyone turned quickly. Vishan stood there. His cloak was hanging from one shoulder, torn to shreds. Blood trickled from a gash in his forehead and he looked unsteady on his feet. He seemed almost embarrassed at having to speak. Parenon and Helen looked at him in silence, realisation and a new, deeper respect beginning to dawn in Parenon's eyes. 'I told him where you were.' Vishan continued. 'It takes more than a grubby group of misfits at the Hunter and Holva to get rid of me!'

The night sky was perfectly clear and the breezes that blew through the camp were crisp and cold. Cleve Harrow, Helen and Parenon sat around the campfire with Tarawen, Sherin and the others. Harrow had told the delighted Helen that her parents were safe. She had learned of their passage to Beltheron and of how eager they were to hear news of her and of how they were preparing to make their own way to Atros to join her.

'…and that will be achieved at first light tomorrow.' The Cleve was still speaking. 'They would have come with me tonight.' He said. 'But I discovered a great setback to our plans and I had to make haste to get here myself. Sherin will stay here to ward you in the Rebel camp, Helen, until your parents arrive down the pathway with more Pulver guards.'

Sherin took a step forwards and bowed his head slightly. There was a look of happy pride on his face.

'What about you and Parenon?' She asked in reply. 'What are *you* going to do?'

'Parenon and I must also stay on Atros. But not here with you in the camp. We have an urgent task.' The Cleve paused for a moment, unsure of how to proceed. 'The setback that I mentioned a moment ago… it is very serious. In fact it could prove the downfall of us all. I am afraid that Jack is in mortal danger. I helped him to escape to Beltheron after the attack on your home, but he was captured by the Rish yesterday evening.'

Helen gasped. 'Oh no! How? Is he alright?' A sharp pain sprang up in her chest. Tears of shock and worry came to her eyes. One part of her mind thought for an instant about how much she had started to care about her cousin in such a short space of time. She realised that his safety was as important to her as her own. She searched Harrow's face for signs of reassurance.

'I believe that he is still alive.' Cleve Harrow put out a hand to comfort her. 'It cannot be doubted, however, that our young friend is now in the clutches of The Wild Lord. With Parenon's help, and that of Tarawen and his rebels, I hope to be able to rescue him.'

'I want to come with you.' Helen said defiantly.

'That cannot be, I am afraid. What would your parents think, when they arrive here tomorrow, to discover that we have led you into even greater peril?'

'They would understand. They would want to do the same thing themselves.' She was defiant.

'It is essential that we do not put you in any further danger.'

'I don't care about that.'

'But I do!'

'I have to do *something*, Cleve!'

Harrow smiled. His voice softened. 'And I do not doubt your bravery my dear girl. But I have to consider the prophesy. You and Jack are tremendously important. I have already failed terribly. Jack is in mortal danger because of me. Me! The very one who should have protected him the most! I should have had more foresight. It is unthinkable that I should make another such mistake. Therefore I cannot risk you both falling into the Wild Lord's clutches. Who knows what terrible uses he would find for you if you both came under his sway.'

Helen knew this made sense. But she had been led to understand from an early age that not only was she important – as the Cleve said – but also that she had a role to play in the history of the three worlds. She felt as if she were ready to fulfil that role *now*, now that there was something vital to be done. It was incredibly frustrating to be told, time and time again, that she must stay out of the way. What was the use of just hiding away? Why couldn't she do something herself? Helen wondered what all her preparation been for if not to be able to do something at times like this? She slumped back against the logs that surrounded the fire, knowing that once again she must do as she was told.

Parenon saw the expression on her face. He went over to her. Bending down he spoke in a low, reassuring voice. 'I know it is difficult. It is courageous and honourable of you to disregard your own safety in favour of helping your cousin. But the Cleve is right. You have a greater part to play. There will be some way for you to help but I do not think that the time has arrived for that yet. Be patient, Lady Yelenia,' - she started at that formal use of her name coming from Parenon – 'your time will come to prove yourself.'

Tarawen appeared next to them. Helen looked up at him and smiled, but saw that he wasn't looking down at her. He was glaring intently into the shadows of the trees close by. His expression made the smile run away from her face. His entire body was tensed with expectation. In the flickering firelight she saw that his eyes were furrowed into grim slits; Parenon had sensed it too and he was already on his feet at Tarawen's side.

'What do you see?'

'Nothing yet, but I thought I heard something a moment ago.'

Parenon squinted into the shadows. Helen got to her feet and followed the direction of his gaze.

'You are right, Tarawen. I think that there *is* something.' He whispered so that even Helen, who was right by his side, could hardly hear him.

'Another pedjiaar, perhaps?'

'Possibly.' Tarawen replied. 'Occasionally they are brave enough to come to the camp – even when there is a fire burning.'

Parenon smiled back at him grimly. 'Brave enough - or hungry enough.'

Both Tarawen and Parenon had their swords in their hands by now. Harrow had gone to talk to some of the other rebels by the fire, but at this moment he looked back towards them. When he saw their expressions and the drawn swords he hurried back towards them.

As soon as he reached them he took Helen by the hand. 'Helen, come with me. If there is danger here then I must insist that…' Harrow's voice stopped suddenly as an arrow caught him on the shoulder. It had a steel shaft with ugly, black feathers at its end. Harrow grunted and fell backwards. Helen cried out in shock and horror.

'Harrow!'

The Cleve struggled to his knees at her side. He clutched at his shoulder. Blood trickled through his fingers. The rebels began to run towards them, drawing their own swords and reaching for their bows.

Suddenly Rish exploded out of the thicket. There were about twenty of them. With the first glance, Parenon saw that only six were mounted on holva; the rest ran rapidly towards them on foot, with clubs and axes in their long arms. Some had up to four weapons each, which they swung from their multiple limbs.

'Bring them down! Bring them down!' Vishan was amongst them now, already notching his bow with a flint tipped arrow. In one fluid movement he brought up the bow to his eye level, pulled the string taught and released it. The string made a throoop! sound as the arrow sped to its target, hitting one of the foremost holva between the eyes. With a deep groan it fell forwards onto its knees. The Rish who had been riding it tumbled over its neck. It fell to the ground and four more rebel arrows pierced its body before it had time to rise.

All around Helen the rebels were running, notching arrows, shouting. Parenon leapt towards the advancing enemy, his own war-cry 'Mage and Council!' ringing out high above the rest of the battle noise.

Five or six Rish had already been felled by the arrows and Parenon himself quickly brought down two more with strong, accurate swings of his sword.

It was not all going the Rebel's way, however. The Rish were now amongst them, swinging their ugly weapons with hatred and deadly malice.

Helen was still by Cleve Harrow's side. He had managed to get to his feet, but he was still clutching his left shoulder and the arm hung uselessly at his side. He had dropped the Golden Staff.

'Helen you must help me. Pick up the staff.' She stooped to do as he said. Close by her, on her right hand side, Helen saw two of the younger rebels that she had been speaking to only that morning. They ran past her, swinging their swords, only to be brought down by a single blow from a long cudgel wielded by the biggest Rish she had yet seen. It turned its egg shaped head towards her with a snarl. The rows of small ugly teeth were flecked with spittle. It raised the club high over her head. There were sickeningly sharp spikes sticking out from it. She winced in anticipation of the crushing blow that she knew must come. But even as the Rish brought down the club she instinctively lifted the Golden Staff to ward off the blow. The Rish club hit the Staff with a jolt that sent Helen onto her knees. There was a searing flash of light and in the same instant the Rish and its club exploded. Sparks scattered on the ground next to her. They fizzed and sputtered on the earth but there was no more sign of the Rish. It had completely vanished.

Helen felt the last of her strength fading. All was noise and confusion and horror around her. She gasped as she felt someone grip her arm tightly. It was Harrow.

'Come Helen. I must transport you from this place.'

The Cleve took the Golden Staff from her. With his one good arm he raised it in front of them both. He was about to create a pathway, Helen realised. But as he did so, both he and Helen were struck by a tremendous force. A holva had hurtled into them. The blow was so devastating that Helen thought a wall must have fallen on top of her, breaking every bone in her body. She was thrown through the air, and away from Harrow. The holva that had charged into them now spun around to face them again. It had no rider. The Rish that had been upon its back now lay dead a few metres away. In pain, fear and rage, the holva now reared over Harrow, stabbing at the air around his head with its broad, skeletal hooves. It was about to plunge forward when the Cleve brought up the Golden Staff yet again. Light burst from the tip, engulfing the holva in a white flash. It vanished. However it seemed that this last effort was too much for the wounded Cleve. He pitched forwards onto his face into the dirt. He lay perfectly still. Helen got to her feet groggily and tried to stagger towards him to help.

'Harrow? Harrow?'

The Cleve did not reply. He did not move. On every side of her, swords clanged on shields, arrows sped to their targets, Rebels and Rish and Holva making a horrible, terrifying noise.

She cried out once more over the din. 'Harrow!' There was no reply. Her cries were all in vain.

Then Helen heard another sound close behind her.

'Heh, heh, heh. So we meet again.'

It was a familiar voice. She turned, and there, grinning evilly at her was Crudpile. Helen opened her mouth to call for help but it was too late. The Cleve was still lying on the ground a few metres away and Parenon was further off in the clearing, battling another Rish as best he could. He had no time to help her now.

Before Helen could run, Crudpile had grasped her arm. She tried to call out but he immediately shoved a filthy hand over her mouth.

'Quiet!' Pinning her with surprising strength, he fumbled in his pocket for a moment before bringing out a small, black vial. Helen's eyes widened in terror. She realised what Crudpile was about to do. She began kicking and screaming even more madly but Crudpile was too strong and he already had the lid off the bottle.

Moments later Harrow staggered to his feet, clutching at his wound. He turned and looked all around him for Helen. By now though, the battle had begun to die down and to his dismay, all signs of Helen and Crudpile had gone.

23

Despair in the Dark

Orianna's head was spinning. Her mother was screaming something in her ear and she had lost her grip on Jack's hand. The darkness was dreadful and the bat's wings beat against her face and drove her to a terrifying panic. She was used to being able to find the answers. Her studies had told her that she could find the truth in her library of books and pamphlets; her books would have the solution to everything. But now she felt betrayed. None of her reading was preparation for this. No matter how she racked her memory, there was nothing to explain what was happening now. Even when they had wandered aimlessly though the corridors she had held out a hope that soon a memory would come to her that would lead to a way out. But it had not come. She was helpless; helpless to assist either herself, her mother, or Jack.

The bats continued to swirl around them, plucking and nipping. Orianna could already feel something warm and wet sliding down her cheek and into the corner of her mouth. With a slide of revulsion in her stomach she knew it was her own blood. The bats would wound them, draw blood, and then feed. A high scream rose above the horrible sounds of the bats. Her mother!

Battling against the swarm of blood bats she made her way towards the sound. She flailed wildly with her hands, panic growing in her. She had lost her grip on her mother's hand! Where had the scream come from? Left and right she reached, all the time feeling the bats grow more numerous around her. As soon as she realised that she was totally alone in the corridor a flash of memory had darted through her head.

It had been long ago. Maybe years. Cleve Harrow's voice was speaking gently to her as she bent over the ancient books in his library. What had he said to her on that day? Something about being alone? Something about comfort and hope? Suddenly the memory came to her, at last, in her final panic, like a beacon of light in the darkness.

'When all else fails you, Orianna, when you feel the most alone, remember this. Words have a power. Whether it is words of lore and wisdom from a book; words of forgotten, favourite stories from our youth; or the remembered words of love from others, they can give you comfort.'

That was it! Words of lore and wisdom! The Cleve had never known about the blood bats, but he had taught her many ancient incantations, words of power and comfort for her darkest hours. She struggled to think. In her mind's eye the image of a leather bound volume appeared. The book seemed to open in front of her and the pages to turn rapidly. Even here, in this dreadful place, the sight of the book, and the memory of the Cleve's words were a comfort. He had been right. When all else fails you, turn to words.

The imaginary pages in front of her had stopped turning over. The book in her mind's eye was now wide open at a particular page. She remembered this book so clearly now. It had all come back to her through the years. Orianna concentrated on the page. She began to read, and then to speak, the ancient words...

Was she dreaming it, or did the poetry of the incantation immediately take away some of the pain and fear? The sound in her ears was like a balm to all of the evil around her. Over and over she repeated the words until they became a soothing lullaby.

As she intoned the words the darkness seemed to recede. The bats stopped their fluttering around her face and she could see her mother's figure huddled down for protection ahead of her. Still speaking the mantra she hurried over to her and picked her up.

The bats had all scattered now. Orianna continued to chant repeatedly, her voice growing more excited as she saw a light appear ahead of them! The glow became more and more distinct as her trembling voice grew stronger with the incantation. The magical words were helping Korellia too; she opened her eyes and looked up into her daughter's face. She took Orianna's hand and squeezed encouragement.

Orianna placed her mother back onto her feet. She staggered slightly, but then found her strength and balance. Hand in hand Orianna and her mother began to make their way out of the tunnels together.

Jack groped his way through the impenetrable dark. It was now over twelve hours since their escape attempt had ended in such terrible failure. But the passage of time meant nothing to Jack in such total blackness. The only way of telling that the time was going by at all was the increasing sense of hunger that he felt. That and the awful parching thirst. He had never felt so thirsty and that was what began to trouble and terrify him the most. What if he *never* found his way out? What if he continued to crawl along in the darkness, all alone, until thirst or sheer exhaustion made him give in to a sleep that would never end? He shuddered. The thought of that was even worse than the threat of capture.

He closed his eyes (not that it made any difference, because he couldn't even see his own hand in front of his face anyway). He thought of how it might have been so different. He had wanted to save Orianna and Korellia so much. He wanted to prove himself; to show everyone that their faith in him was justified.

But it wasn't justified. He knew that now. He had failed them. He hated to think of what fate must have befallen them down in those terrible caverns. Why had he let go of her hand? The last thing he remembered was Orianna's terrified cry as they were separated. And those bats! The recollection of the screeching sound they made and the horrible fluttering of their wings against his face gave him a strange lurch in his stomach. His eyes shot open again. There was a dim red light in the corner of his vision. A light! But it wasn't ordinary light. He slowly realised that it was the same strange, red glow that he had first seen through the windows of Matt and Jenn's house, when he had sensed that something terrible was going to happen. This time the red glow seemed to be coming from down the corridor. He wiped tears from his eyes. 'Now what?' he thought to himself. Jack struggled to his feet. He wasn't going to give up. That would be an insult to Orianna and Korellia, and the Cleve, who had done so much for him. Starved, battered and exhausted, Jack staggered down the corridor in the direction of the glowing red light...

Helen clung on to Crudpile as the swirling torrents of the pathway spun around her. Where in the three worlds was he taking her?

As soon as she asked herself the question she realised

the answer. Crudpile was going to get his reward after all. He would take her straight to Gretton Tur. There would be no escape this time. Bitterly, Helen thought just how close she had been to safety. Crudpile's claw-like fingers gripped her shoulder viciously. It occurred to Helen that if she let go, if she pushed herself away from his grip, she would be torn away from him by the force of the Pathway. It would fling her outwards into oblivion. 'At least that way would be a quick death' she considered. Tur would win anyway, she knew that now. He held Jack as a prisoner already. Soon she would join him in the dungeons, if he wasn't dead already. Who knew what tortures The Wild Lord had in store?

The Pathway continued to spin around her. The force that was holding and carrying them was incredible. If she did let go she would be sucked out and dissolve in an instant. It would certainly be quick. 'It would be so easy.' She thought. 'Let go. Just do it. At least this villain will be cheated of his reward.' But even as she felt her fingers loosening around Crudpile's waist and the power of the Pathway tugging at her limbs, she realised that was not the way. She would not give them the satisfaction of thinking that she had given up, given in to them. 'No! I am a Select of Beltheron! I will struggle and fight for all I am worth. I will not give in!' She clung on even more tightly as the Pathway streamed past.

The sound in her ears reached a crescendo and she felt them slowing down. There was a juddering sensation through her knees and she realised that they had arrived.

The white glow around her disappeared. She saw that she and Crudpile were standing in the Gretton Tur's throne room. There he sat, on his black, carved seat of power. He grinned at her and Helen felt the blood go cold in her veins. Just the sight of The Wild Lord was worse than anything she had imagined. 'Why didn't I let go of Crudpile when I had the chance?' she thought.

'Hello my dear.' Gretton Tur said in his gravel-like voice. 'So nice of you to visit.'

The red light in front of Jack was growing much brighter as he drew closer. There was something important there, he knew it. He remembered that back on earth, when he had arrived at Matt and Jenn's house, the glowing in the windows had been a warning of the Rish. Later, when he and Orianna were in the Beltheron market place he realised that the red flash he had seen in the corner of his eye was not just a reflected beam of sunlight. It was a signal, no – more than that, a premonition, for him to turn around and see the Shifter. And now, when he looked back on it, he also recognised that the red glow from Korellia's fire later that night had seemed just a little bit too bright. Moments later, the Shifter had returned and started snuffling at their door. If only he had realised earlier that these glowing, red glares were an indication that something important was about to happen, then he might have been able to avert the disaster with the bats. Once again he punished himself with the guilty idea that it was his fault Orianna and Korellia were probably dead.

He shook his head grimly. It was no use thinking like that. He would only despair of all hope if he carried on dwelling on it. He stumbled on.

Up ahead of him, just at a slight turn in the corridor, the light grew brighter still for just a moment. Then it began to fade away. Just before he was plunged back into total darkness he caught a glimpse of something different in the shape of the left hand wall up ahead. It seemed to be a slightly different colour and texture to the rest of the stone wall. Not like stone at all, but more like a dull fabric. Why would there be fabric hanging there? His mind raced. A wall hanging? That made no sense down in those tunnels. A curtain? Why have a curtain unless it was covering a window? No! Not a window, but maybe a door! He tried to fix the position of it in his mind's eye. He made a guess that it must have been about ten paces in front of him. Jack walked carefully towards the place on the wall, counting his footsteps under his breath. Jack had to find his way by feeling along the wall for the last few faltering steps. It had been here somewhere, he *knew* it. He ran his fingers across the cold, rough stone. There was nothing except the harsh grating feel of the rock. He took another pace forwards, still feeling his way. He must have reached it by now, he was certain that it hadn't been so far ahead, but there was still no indication of anything different in the wall. Maybe he had just imagined it after all. His last despairing hopes had tricked him into thinking that there was some chance for him. But no, he *knew* that there *had* been something there. Perhaps he had missed it? 'Just a couple of paces more.' He told himself. 'Then I'll double back and check again.'

He felt so tense that he was hardly even breathing. Another step. He felt all around the wall as far as he could reach. Nothing. A final step. Still nothi... wait! The tips of his fingers touched a ragged piece of cloth. At the same moment he sensed a slight breeze blow against his cheek. He gulped it in. It was the freshest air that he had felt ever since they had been thrown into the dungeons.

Jack's heart started to hammer with excitement. With his ears alert to the slightest warning sound he pulled gently at the fabric.

The curtain opened easily. It felt brittle under his fingers as he moved it. He groped behind the curtain. There was a door. He moved his hands more swiftly now, trying to find some kind of handle or catch.

There it was! A cold, round metal handle under his fingers. He concentrated all his attention upon the handle and turned it. It gave a gentle creak and the door swung open in front of him. His heart was pounding even more violently, but there was no sound in the room beyond so he took a step into the darkness.

As soon as he was fully inside the room he felt a sensation that was beginning to feel familiar to him. Just at the corner of his eye-line he could see a red glowing light, what he now thought of as his built-in alarm that something dangerous was about to happen. He wouldn't ignore it this time. He stepped quickly and quietly to one side. The red glow was getting brighter. He could now see an outlandish figure leaning against the wall, illuminated by the red glimmer. Jack's heart stopped with terror. It was a Rish guard!

Jack stood there motionless. The Rish was holding a large shield and a long, curved blade. Its mouth was opened slightly in a frightening grimace. Jack could see the long rows of serrated teeth. Its eyes were wide open but looked blank and still. The Rish was bending towards him, as if to make out his whereabouts in the dim light. It would surely see him in a moment. It was only a couple of metres away, how could it *not* see him?

The seconds ticked by. The Rish did not move. Its eyes continued to glare out blankly in Jack's direction. The sword remained in an upright position, grasped in one of the hooked upper hands. Still it did not move towards him. 'Please!' thought Jack. 'Do something, just get it over with!'

Then another thought struck him. There was something wrong about the blankness of those eyes;

something unnatural about the angle that the Rish was managing to maintain.

Taking all of his courage into his hands, Jack moved slightly to his left. The Rish stayed where it was. Jack moved again, more swiftly this time. He raised his arms in front of him. The Rish stood there, motionless.

A grin began to form on Jack's lips. He waved his hands in front of the horrible face that was leering down at him. It ignored him. He jumped up and down in front of the creature. It didn't move. Finally he reached out and touched the Rish on one of its lower arms. It was cold.

Jack breathed out in a long drawn out sigh. The Rish was dead.

24

The Plan Revealed

Jack had been running for some time. Since finding the dead Rish guarding the doorway he had not looked back. He now knew which way to go. It was as if the breath in his nostrils was getting cleaner every moment. On through the corridors he races until he was sure he must have been close to the dungeons again. From there he knew he could soon find his way back to the surface.

Suddenly he stopped in his tracks. The sound of a frightened scream had split the air in front of him. He knew the voice. Helen! She was here in this awful place as well! He heard the scream again. It came from just around the corner. It seemed to Jack she was very close indeed. Slowing his pace he made his way around the next corner. He kept to the shadows along the wall. Now he could hear other voices as well. They were laughing and jeering; taunting poor Helen.

The voices made Jack furious. "Why can't they just leave us alone?" he thought to himself. Then he heard something that made him halt in his tracks. He thought he heard one of the guards saying something about sending for her cousin? Did this mean that they still didn't know that he had escaped form the dungeon with Orianna and Korellia? Perhaps that gave him a few minutes of extra advantage. Just a few minutes before they went to get him and discovered his disappearance. He peered around the corner just in time to see the guards shamble off up the corridor. He waited a few more moments until he was sure that they had gone.

Jack crept forwards. He could hear Helen's lonely sniffles as she tried not to give in to tears. The sound almost broke Jack's heart.

'Helen!' he hissed under his breath.

The crying sounds stopped suddenly. He thought he heard his cousin gasp in surprise. He called again. 'Helen?'

'Jack! Is that you?'

'I'm coming to get you. Stay where you are.'

'Where do you think I'm going to go? I'm locked up in a cell for goodness' sake!'

He turned the corner and there she was in front of him. He grinned with delighted relief at the sight of her.

'Don't worry about that. Locks don't seem to be much of a problem for me these days.'

As Jack ran down the corridor towards her cell he held out his hand – palm forwards - in front of him. By the time he had reached the cell door the bolt had slid back of its own accord and Helen was already pushing the door open.

'Hey cousin, you're getting good at this!' She smiled widely at him. 'You might even become a fully fledged member of a Select family at this rate. Even if you are still rubbish with a Kron!'

Before, this would have hurt Jack's feelings immensely. But now he grinned back, able to share the joke. The relief at freeing Helen had even made the horrors of the last hours fade a little.

'Come on. We don't have long before they come back.' Jack urged her along the corridor. 'This is the way out isn't it?'

'I think so,' Helen began to say, 'at least this is the way that they brought me down from the…'

Her voice faltered as they heard footsteps around the corner ahead, coming rapidly towards them. They glanced at each other, then around at the walls. There was no doorway or alcove to hide in. The footsteps were getting closer. Helen turned and looked back the way that they had just come. They had already run some distance from the dungeon and the tunnel ran straight all the way. It was no use running back that way; they would be seen before they reached a bend. There was no escape. They would have to face whoever was approaching.

Instinctively Jack reached for Helen's hand. She looked at him with a grim smile, trying to encourage him that things would still be alright, even though she herself was quaking with fear inside. As Jack reached for his sword a boy appeared around the corner. He stopped in his tracks as he saw them.

As they looked closer at the boy they realised that he was probably only about their own age. Despite this he was at least a head taller than either Jack or Helen. He stood proudly with his head erect, staring back at them. His hair was long and fair, and he had bright blue eyes. There was a thick leather belt around his waist. It held a scabbard and a long sword. The boy was moving his fingers lightly over the carving on the sword's handle as he glared at them spitefully. Jack didn't like the look of that sword at all. Still, someone ought to say *something*.

Jack cleared his throat. 'Who are you?' His mouth was dry and his voice came out all wrong, like a squeak.

The other boy just laughed, and twirled his hand more purposefully around the handle of his sword.

'Who am I?' he replied at last, in a calm and level voice which showed he felt much more in control of the situation than Jack did. 'My name?' He paused briefly as he looked at Jack as if to savour this moment. 'My name is *Jacques Andressen*! Son of Piotre and Sofia Andressen, twenty-third generation of the Select of Beltheron! That is who *I* am! So, the question that really needs to be answered is, who are *you*?'

His final words came out in a venomous rush of pure sneering hatred. He glared at Jack, and then at Helen, whose mouth was hanging wide open in disbelief.

Jack was completely stunned for a moment. Then he thought, 'This is just a trick, he's trying to throw me off my guard.'

'You're lying!' he shouted at the boy. 'I am Jacques Andresen. You are just trying to trick us!'

'Am I?' came the jeering reply. 'Think about it, Gutter Boy. Who could be better for Gretton Tur to train as an accomplice than one who already has *real* power, *real* magic flowing through his veins? Who could be better to help him in his grand design to achieve power over the mighty Select than a member of the Select themselves?' The boy was slowly circling Jack and Helen now. His fingers still played around the sword handle. They both turned, to keep their eyes fixed on him. Eventually Helen spoke. 'But, that can't be right. You *are* lying, you must be. This,' she pointed at Jack, '*this* is Jacques Andressen. He has the powers of the Select, he can open doors and locks, and... and...' she began fumbling for words.

'And what else?' asked the stranger. 'Nothing but that? The *real* Jacques would have more abilities than that. Gutter Boy here must have been given a Kron to play with, surely?' he went on sarcastically; 'has he ever managed to use it successfully?'

Neither Jack nor Helen replied to this. Both of them were full of the horror that what this arrogant young man was saying might have some truth in it.

The boy calling himself Jacques continued. 'As I said before, a twenty-third generation Select who was trained by Gretton Tur from childhood would be a mighty foe, a dreadful warrior. Kidnapping me and bringing me here to Atros was the easy part. The only problem was how to keep it secret from that old fool Ungolin, and his lap-dog, Harrow.' Still circling, the boy now had his hand clenched tight around the sword. Jack's own fingers were centimetres above the buckle that held his own sword in its sheath. The buckle twitched and slowly started to unfasten itself under his hand.

'Oh, not yet, not yet, Gutter Boy. Although I must admit that's a neat little trick. But first, don't you want to know how Gretton Tur managed to get me to Atros without anyone noticing?'

A cold shiver ran down the length of Helen's spine. She gasped as the truth dawned on her. The sudden realisation of what must have happened eleven years ago struck her like a heavy blow to her stomach. Her voice came out in a whisper; she was almost speaking to herself. 'You were switched.' She said. She continued speaking slowly as it all worked itself out in her head. 'For the plan to work, no one must realise that Jacques Andressen had been brought here to Atros. The best way to keep the secret would be if no one *even realised that he had gone!* The real Jacques Andressen needed to be replaced. So you two were switched! They swapped you for him! Of course!' Jack turned his attention away from the stranger to look at her, still not understanding. Helen gazed back at him, her face ashen with shock, and her mouth hanging open. There were tears in her eyes. 'Oh Jack, I'm so sorry. Don't you see? Don't you see what they did?'

Jack didn't see, not yet. But there was something in

the back of his mind about how he had always felt as if he was being not just looked after, but *guarded* by his mum and dad, and by Larena their house sitter. Then, other thoughts started to swarm into his imagination; all the time his parents had spent away on business; the fact that he *couldn't* make the Kron work; and the story told to him by a white-haired woman, about the abduction of her son, one night almost twelve years ago…

His thoughts were interrupted by the sneering voice once more. 'I think you're starting to get the idea, aren't you.'

The boy calling himself Jacques Andressen was getting closer, step by deliberate step. The tip of his sword made small circles in the air in front of him as he advanced.

'Let me explain it simply. Your friend here is right. She is obviously much cleverer than you - although of course that is not saying much. She has guessed perfectly correctly. You and I *were* switched. I was taken to Gretton Tur, to begin my training, and you were taken from your own home, Korellia's home, and put in my place.'

And now of course the dreadful truth dawned on Jack in a blinding flash. 'Korellia's baby!' he whispered. 'The baby who was stolen by the Rish. That was me!'

His adversary laughed cruelly. 'Ha haah! That's it gutter boy! Got it in one! Congratulations. You're the son of that worthless street peddler. A nobody. That's why you were chosen to replace me. After a little while no one would bother to look for you or even wonder too much about your fate. And that was all that was needed. You were just an ordinary child whom everyone would soon forget; the perfect replacement for me.'

'You are Korellia's son.' Helen said. 'You're not Jack Anders, you're Serrion Melgardes.'

Jack – or Serrion – went dizzy. He felt as if someone

had pulled the carpet from under his feet. So many ideas swirled in his head he could hardly concentrate on what was being said to him. If he really *were* Serrion Melgardes, then surely his parents must have known about the switch. Even though they had never seemed to take much interest in him they *must* have realised that he was suddenly a different baby. So they *must* have been involved. Jack/Serrion knew in a blinding flash that the two people he had always thought of as his parents were the enemy. His mum and dad were the spies who had been helping Gretton Tur to open the pathways to Beltheron and to Earth. *They* had sent him to stay with Uncle Matt, Aunt Jenn and Helen so that all four of them would be together under the same roof. His parents must have faked their own mysterious disappearance and ransacked their own home in London to make it look like another Rish attack. In that way, when the Rish attacked Matt and Jenn's house that same night, Peter and Sophie knew that they would not be suspected. They could then reappear at some later date, probably with some fantastic story about bravely escaping from Gretton Tur, and carry on betraying Cleve Harrow, Ungolin and all the rest. They would probably be trusted all the more, and pitied because everyone would believe they had lost their own son to the Wild Lord.

Jack/Serrion felt his head swim with it all.

'Understand now, Gutter Boy?' Jacques laughed at him. 'Brilliant little plan wasn't it. And do you know the best of it? That idiot Ungolin never even guessed. He made it all so easy. Over the years I have been prepared by my Master, the Wild lord. He has readied me for the battle to come, and never once have I been bothered by Ungolin's meagre attentions. He doesn't even know that I exist.' The boy who was the real Jacques stepped forwards once more, and the circling blade made a quick, cutting motion towards his adversary. 'That is now about to change. Your part in all of this is no longer necessary. You have played your part and I will now take great pleasure in *killing you!*' As he spat out the final two words he lunged forwards. Jacques thrust his sword at Jack/Serrion. He had just enough time to step aside, but the point of the blade lodged in his tunic, ripping it open. He and Helen turned and without a word to each other, sped off as one.

Down the corridor they ran, Jacques at their heels. His infernal taunting laughter rang in their ears all the way down into the depths of Tur's castle. Neither knew which way they were heading, to safety and a way out, or deeper into another trap. Suddenly they reached a turning where the corridor widened to make room for two other doorways on either side. Now, for the first time in the chase it was just wide enough for Jack/Serrion to swing his sword. Spinning on his heel, he brought the heavy blade upwards as swiftly as he could. He leaned backwards as he spun around, and using the momentum of his turn, he managed to make the blade whistle quickly through the air up towards Jacques' shoulder. But Jacques was even swifter. His blade was already held aloft to parry Jack's swing. The two swords clanged together loudly and bright sparks shot from the steel. It was almost as if he had seen the move Jack had intended before he had even begun to make it.

Jacques laughed again. 'You see? No training, Gutter Boy! Now let me show you what a *real* warrior can do.' His sword was already coming down in a blur towards Jack's head. Jack stepped back, throwing his weight to one side so that Jacques' sword missed him by a centimetre. Like lightning Jacques swung again. Jack was off balance now, but his sword was still raised from his last move and somehow it stopped the blow with another clash of sparks. Jacques fury was increasing with every second. He had expected this to be an easy contest, and was growing impatient with the battle. Jacques was sure that this shred of a boy could not defend himself for much longer however, and he swung his sword at Jack again and again and again...

25
Inside and Out

Out on the plain, Parenon was rallying his soldiers. The Rish were almost defeated. Wave upon wave had stormed from Gretton Tur's castle and out onto the plain in front of the city. But the blasts from the staves of the soldiers held them back, while Parenon and his companions ran among them, slicing and chopping with their swords. The Pulver had suffered many injuries themselves, but it seemed that the Rish were weakening and the Pulver were gaining the upper hand.

But now Gretton Tur himself strode out onto the battlements. He held the Black Staff high above his head, and with a dreadful cry he soared into the air and entered the fray. Blistering white bolts of energy shot from the Black Staff. They knocked riders from their horses as he flew above them, blew apart fighting men and Rish, and shattered the Beltheron weapons. Parenon paused for a moment and gazed up in terrified awe at the Wild Lord, revealed now in all his fury. The sight almost made Parenon falter, but then he became even more determined. 'Now we *must* take him!' He said to himself grimly. 'This is our final chance. But we need to all work together. If only I can gather enough men onto the higher ground over there...' A knock on his shoulder interrupted his thoughts. It brought him back to the immediate reality of his fight with the Rish. He gathered his wits again just in time to parry a fierce lunge from a slobbering, axe-wielding demon. Leaping sideways,

Parenon plunged his sword into the creature, running it through. Then with a loud cry of 'For Mage and Council, to me! To me!' he turned and began to run to the higher, raised ground not far from the centre of the battlefield.

The soldiers heard his cry. Battling their way through the throng they made their slow, dangerous way to follow their Captain. High above them, hovering in the smoky skies, Gretton Tur also heard this new rallying call of Parenon's, and he curved around in the air. His black cloak billowed around him like vast ugly wings and Gretton Tur descended like a bird of prey upon the soldiers of Beltheron…

Jack knew that he was tiring. The fight had gone on too long. He and Helen had been driven back down the staircase, and were now outside the open gates of a cell. Jacques' taunting continued.

'I have just been playing until now. You think that your petty skills are a match for true power. Well watch this!' As he spoke his hand shot out, pointing his sword directly at Helen. Light like orange liquid fire shot from the end of the sword straight at her head. Jack cried out with fury and raced towards Jacques, but he was too late. Behind him he heard Helen scream out in pain and fear as the fiery bolts hit her. He ploughed on into his enemy, ducking under Jacques' raised sword-arm and barging him with his shoulder to try to knock him off balance. At the same time he raised his own sword again to strike. Even now Jacques was too quick. He brought his flaming sword around to counter the blow. Their weapons met with a dull clang. Jack felt the blow jolt pain right up into his shoulder. Jacques' other hand was already reaching under Jack's sword arm. Jacques twisted violently, throwing all his force and weight into the manoeuvre, and swung Jack into the wall. Poor Jack felt the sharp sting of the rough rock as it scraped down the side of his face, stunning him and grazing away a deep layer of flesh. A smear of blood ran down the wall. With what felt like his final ounce of strength, Jack swung his sword handle into Jacques' nose. There was a single dull, snapping sound. Jacques grunted and staggered backwards. He stumbled on the steps behind him and fell heavily to the ground, striking his head on the stone. 'Got him! I got him!' Jack thought to himself. Then he collapsed to his knees and his vision began to fade. The last thing he saw as he fell forwards was Helen's crumpled body on the ground next to him; sparks and ripples of orange fire still curling around her head...

Parenon heard a whooshing rush of air just above him. The sky went dark and there was a beating sound like heavy wings. He spun around. There, hovering close to the ground was Gretton Tur. His black stave was pointing straight at Parenon's chest. A jet of green fire shot from the end of the stave and struck Parenon's sword. The sword shattered into a thousand fragments and Parenon was twisted around and hurled backwards through the air. He landed on his side with a heavy thud that took the breath from his lungs. His head swam with pain and shock. Parenon had never known a force as powerful as this. Before he had time to shake his head to clear it of the stars that were swirling in front of his eyes, the dark shape of Gretton Tur was hovering above him again. Once more the Wild Lord brandished his black stave, this time pointing it straight at Parenon's unprotected head. Parenon scrabbled around in the dirt for something, anything at all that he could use as a weapon, but there was no discarded sword, no rocks to throw, not even gravel to hurl into the eyes of the Wild Lord. The black stave was only inches in front of him and Gretton Tur was leering cruelly. Parenon closed his eyes and waited for the burst of fire that he knew would come at any moment.

There was a sudden flash of light, so bright that it stung his eyes even though they were tightly closed. 'Here it is,' thought Parenon, 'the moment of my death.' A scream filled his ears, but it was not his own voice. Cautiously he opened his eyes. Gretton Tur still hovered above his prone body, but he had undergone an amazing transformation. The Wild Lord was encircled with a ring of bright white light and he was twisting and writhing in agony. Parenon realised that the white flame that held Gretton Tur was coming from just behind his own shoulder. He turned himself around and saw Cleve Harrow, standing tall and straight, holding the Golden Staff of Beltheron firmly in both hands. The staff pointed directly at Gretton Tur, and the bolts of light that sprang from its tip were slowly blasting the Wild Lord of Atros into oblivion. As Parenon watched, Tur's grip on the Black Stave grew weaker and weaker, until he let it go with a long, bone-wrenching shriek: 'Nooo!' Instead of falling to the ground the Black Stave shot up into the air and sped through the clouds in the direction of the Palace. Parenon could see that Harrow was beginning to tire. He started to stagger, and his grip on the Golden Staff was not as sure and steady as it had been a few moments ago. The Cleve's teeth were clenched tight, but Parenon could make out that he was trying to speak. His voice came out in a croaking whisper. 'Almost…there. He…tires. But I… I… weaken also.' Cleve Harrow looked at Parenon and summoned his last ounces of breath. 'Finish him!'

Parenon nodded briefly at Harrow. He looked around on the ground near to his feet and saw a discarded blade only a few metres away; dropped by a wounded Pulver. He staggered towards it, moving as quickly as his punished, battered body would allow. The blade was heavy as he picked it up, but it seemed to give him a new strength. Parenon turned purposefully back to where Harrow was still holding Gretton Tur in the fiery grip of the Golden Staff.

'Hurry!' Groaned Harrow. 'I cannot hold him.'

Parenon shifted his grip so that he could hold the sword with both hands. He glared directly into the Wild Lord's eyes. The fury and hatred that he saw there was so intense that it made him quail and falter for a moment. Only for a moment however. He raised his weapon and thrust it firmly into Gretton Tur's breast. Throwing all of his weight behind the blow he felt the sword sink into the Wild Lord's body right up to the hilt. Gretton Tur shrieked in fury and pain. The light from the Golden Staff now encircled all three of the embattled figures. Cleve Harrow stood with the Staff still pointing its fire at Tur, who was now shaking violently in the air. Parenon had been driven to his knees. He was directly underneath Tur, his strength all but spent, but still working his sword backwards and forwards in Tur's body. The shrieking continued as Tur seemed to dwindle and collapse inside his cloak.

At the edge of the battle plain, the Palace of Gendrell began to shake. The topmost towers shivered in a way similar to the trembling and shaking of Gretton Tur's own body. Then the black stones and slates of the towers started to crumble and fall into the courtyards below.

'That's it!' Harrow screamed over the cacophony of sounds. 'We have him! Keep working your blade!'

Parenon glanced up at the palace. As he did, the stones from high up on one of the larger towers exploded outwards, and one of the main supporting walls collapsed.

'It is only being held together by his will! Parenon, take off his mangy head!'

Parenon withdrew his sword and staggered back onto his feet. Tur's body was still shaking violently, uncontrollably. Parenon took a deep breath into his lungs and swung the sword around in a high, wide arc. In one clean blow, it severed the head of Gretton Tur, the Wild Lord of Atros. Even before it had fallen to the ground, the head, the body and the black cloak had all vanished in a dark cloud of thick smoke...

Helen realised that she was lying on hard stone. The rumbling sound in the palace seemed distant in her ears at first. But it grew louder and louder. The ground under her started to tremble and dust began to fall from the ceiling above her head. She tried to push herself into a sitting position but as soon as she moved a piercing agony hit her behind her eyes. The memories began to come back to her slowly. Jack had been fighting with someone. No. Not Jack. The person whom she knew as Jack was really someone else. Was that right? Was that what had happened? She tried hard to remember. Jack was Serrion? Serrion was Jack? She shook her head to clear the confusion. Ouch! That was a mistake. More pain shot through her temples. Stupid! Stupid! Stupid! She told herself. The rumbling noise around her was getting louder. What *was* that? Moving very carefully so as not to jolt more pain into her delicate head she looked around her. There was her cousin, Jack - or Serrion - propped up next to the wall of the corridor. A few yards away another boy lay flat on his back. Suddenly it all came back to her. This *second* boy was really her cousin, Jacques Andresen. Both boys seemed to be unconscious. Helen dragged herself over to Jack/Serrion. The ground underneath them was shaking quite violently now. Pieces of masonry began to fall from above.

She gently shook the shoulders of the boy who was really Serrion Melgardes. He groaned and opened his eyes.

'Helen? Is that you?'

'Yes, it's me. Listen there's no time to explain anything, but we have to get out of here as quickly as we can.'

There was another loud rumble and more dust and heavy chunks of masonry came crashing down, only just missing them both.

'Do you think you can stand?' Helen asked him, ignoring the pain that was still digging into the back of her own eyes.

'Yes, I think so.'

She helped him stagger to his feet.

'Where is Jacques?' he asked as Helen took his arm.

'I am behind you, gutter boy!' The familiar voice spun both of them around. Jacques Andresen had also managed to stand. He still held onto his sword, and even though he looked unsteady on his feet, he was advancing slowly towards them. 'There's no escape for either of you this time. You are about to die!'

A louder crash suddenly rent the air and echoes – or aftershocks – sounded from other parts of the palace.

'You must stop this!' Helen yelled at him. 'If we don't get out of here in the next few minutes we will *all* die!'

'I don't think so, cousin!' he spat the word at her with hatred. Jacques raised his sword 'This will only take me a moment and then I will...' his words were cut short as the ground lurched under their feet. Jack/Serrion saw his chance. He leapt forwards. His hand grabbed Jacques sword arm, thrusting it upwards and away from Helen. At the same moment he pushed Jacques backwards into the wall. Helen bent to pick up the fallen sword. Jacques had recovered his balance and was about to chop at him again, but Helen was there in time, she parried the blow and knocked Jacques' weapon from his hand. Jacques screamed in fury. Behind him was a cell. The door was gaping wide open. Jack/Serrion continued to push forwards until he forced Jacques into the cell. With a final heave he managed to separate himself from his opponent and step backwards. Helen's hand shot out and light flared from her fingertips. The jolt shot Jacques further back into the cell.

'You're not the only one who can make fireworks, *cousin*!' she yelled. Jack/Serrion flung himself at the door and the heavy metal clanged shut.

'I can't do fireworks like you, but just wait until you see this!' he said to Helen with a grin. He spread his fingers out a few centimetres from the cell door lock. With a grinding sound the metal began to meld itself together, sealing the door closed with Jacques trapped inside.

'Pretty good, eh?' he said to Helen.

She grinned back. 'Not bad – for a beginner.'

'Open this door! Open this DOOR!' Jacques' voice ripped through his clenched teeth with terrifying hatred.

The floor lurched under them again. Serrion and Helen looked at each other, and then back at the boy in the cell. They hesitated. The rumbling grew more violent.

'We haven't got time to do anything for him.' Helen made the decision for both of them. 'We have to get out.'

She turned to run back up the corridor. Still Jack/ Serrion hesitated. To leave Jacques here was as bad as killing him.

'Come on!' Helen pleaded. 'He was about to kill us both a few moments ago. He still would if he had a chance.'

As if to prove Helen's point another sharp stab of fire hit the wall next to their heads. Jacques was reaching through the bars of the cell with one arm, firing bolts of fury at them.

'See what I mean?' she yelled over the crashing. 'We have got to go now!'

He realised that there was nothing else to do. He turned to follow her out of the dungeons as the walls of the palace crumbled around them. Bereft of the power of Gretton Tur, the building was collapsing in on itself. Behind them, Jacques voice could still be heard calling out vengeance. 'I won't forget this, Gutter Boy! Cousin Helen! I will find you, and when I do you will both pay. You will pay more dearly than you can ever imagine!'

Jack and Helen ran on. They reached a curving staircase cut out of the rock of the cellars. The steps wound up and out of sight around a corner. Next to it was another staircase leading down into the darkness. There was no doubt which way to go.

They hurled themselves up the staircase with what remained of their strength. As they climbed, more rocks fell. Clouds of dust made it difficult for them to see. They both kept flinching as they expected to be hit by a rock at any moment. Once, out of the fog of dust, Helen thought she saw something long and black whiz past her ear and back down the staircase the way that they had just climbed up. On and on, up and up wound the stair, with uneven steps throwing them off balance and constantly threatening to trip them.

Up ahead, around the curve of the stair Jack thought that he heard a new sound; a sudden fluttering, flapping noise. He stopped so abruptly that Helen bumped into him from behind. He motioned with his hand for her to be still and silent for a moment. He was still holding his sword after his battle with Jacques. Raising it in front of him he cautiously climbed the next few stairs, slowly rounding the corner. The flapping sound had stopped. Helen followed him silently.

Just ahead of them at the top of the steps sat a large black raven. It did not move. It held both of them in its cold, blank stare. The raven tilted its head to one side, as if it were wondering about something.

'It's only a bird.' Said Helen. 'Come on, it can't hurt us. We've got to get out.'

She made a move to pass Jack on the stairs. There was something about the bird that made Jack hesitate. Something was not quite right. A dim memory came to him. He had seen a bird like this somewhere before.

Helen was drawing closer to the Raven. It still hadn't moved but it was watching her closely.

'Shoo!' she flapped her arms at the bird. It did not move. 'Go on, shoo I say!'

'Helen, I wouldn't do that if I were you.'

'Don't be silly, we have to get out of here.'

'I know, but there's something odd about this bird. Please, Helen. Don't get any closer.'

The bird cocked its head to the other side, but still made no other movement. Helen stepped towards it, making the shooing motions again.

'I will not be stopped by a stupid little...ouch!'

As Helen took a final step towards it the bird lashed out suddenly with its beak, nipping her savagely on the back of her hand. She drew it back quickly in pain and surprise. It lashed out again, stabbing violently at her ankles. Helen kicked at it in disgust. 'Get away from me you silly thing. We don't want to hurt you. We just want to get out of here. You'd better fly off yourself if you don't want to get tra...'

Helen stopped speaking and her mouth hung open in amazement. Jack was now at the top of the staircase too. He also stared at the bird, unable to believe his eyes.

The raven had begun to grow. It was already three

times its original size. In a few moments more it was the size of an eagle. But that was not the only change. The raven's legs had started to lengthen and get thicker, and there was a sickening cracking sound as its wings spread and elongated. It was now shedding feathers from all over its body and out of its head in their place grew long, wiry black hairs. The creature was now so big that it blocked the staircase. They could not get past it. Jack was so stunned that he could not move.

The bird was now recognisable as a human form. The beak formed a hooked nose and the tiny, cold eyes were growing larger under thick black eyebrows. There was something very familiar about the creature that Jack could not quite put his finger on.

Then, as the creature continued to change, he realised with a jolt who it was.

'Larena!'

'What?' Helen said, unable to take her eyes from what was happening.

Jack stood up straight. The transformation was almost complete now. There could be no more mistaking the hateful figure in front of him.

'It is you, isn't it, Larena?' His words came out in a cold, flat tone.

The bird/woman cackled.

'Yes. It's me. Lovely to see you again Ja... Oh, but you've probably found out by now. Let's finish with all that pretence. Not Jack any longer. Allow me to call you *Master Serrion Melgardes!*'

As she spoke, Jack and Helen noticed her tongue. The rest of her had finished changing now, the feathers replaced by a black, leathery looking garment. But her tongue...her tongue was still the tongue of a bird, small and hard and dark. It kept flicking quickly in and out of Larena's mouth as she spoke. Helen thought that she was going to be sick.

'All those years looking after you, boy, and you have no word of welcome for your old babysitter?'

The words were cruel and teasing.

'Come, come,' she continued, slowly moving towards them. 'That is most impolite. What would your mother and father say? Oh, but there I go again! They're *not* your mother and father, are they? Your real father died a long time ago. I should know.' She paused for a moment and looked straight at Jack. 'I should know because it was me who killed him!' With these words Larena shot forwards. She struck Helen across the face with one hand, knocking her aside as she lunged for Jack.

'You never suspected me of being a breed of Shifter, did you?' Larena continued. The teasing tone had gone from her voice. She was spitting the words at him now. Jack was being forced to go backwards down the steps, the way they had just come.

'The Wild Lord offered me power,' she continued; 'power to choose an animal form in return for assisting him.'

She raked her hands towards him. Jack noticed her long sharp nails. They came to a point, and were hard and curved like a bird of prey's talons.

'Of course, I was only too happy to oblige him.'

He was still descending the steps, his sword wavering in front of him. Focusing on Larena, he was unsure of how or where to strike. Helen was creeping up behind her now, Jack saw. She was raising her hand towards Larena's back. Out of the corner of his eye he saw the concentration gather in Helen's face as she prepared to send out a bolt of flame towards the bird-woman. In the same instant Larena whirled around and leapt into the air. The black leathery fabric of her clothing swirled about her and she kicked out, knocking Helen to the floor. Larena hovered easily for a moment and then sank back gracefully to the ground, completely unnerved. Jack finally saw his chance. Driven to further rage at the sight of Helen being kicked, he yelled out in fury, leaping forwards, his sword straight out in front of him. How dare she do that to Helen! But Larena was still too quick for him. Merely stepping aside and turning again, she used Jack's own forward momentum to hurl him head over heels along the corridor. The sword flew from his hands and skittered across the floor, completely out of his reach. Helen was still struggling to her feet, dazed as the palace continued to shake all around them. Larena stepped up to Jack.

'I have played games with you long enough. You have bored me for twelve years. Having to keep my eye on you was the worst part of all my service to the Wild Lord.' The hatred in her features was terrifying. She advanced on Jack, raising both hands with those hideous claws, ready to strike the final blow. 'But no longer. You and your kind, the pathetic Select, may strive for victory, but you will never defeat us in the end. And the end has come for you NOW!'

As she leapt towards him there was an eruption of light. Jack could not tell where it had come from. He watched from the floor as the light enveloped Larena in mid-air. It turned her around as if she were a spinning top. Her arms flailed around and an anguished shriek came from her lips. The light all around her was glowing brighter and brighter all the time. It was now a fiery orange. The scream coming from Larena had reached such a pitch that it seemed completely inhuman. Jack covered his ears. He twisted himself around on the ground to try to see where the flame was coming from.

Uncle Matt and Auntie Jenn were standing a few metres away. Jenn held both her arms out towards Larena's spinning body. In her hands she held a small globe. The light was streaming from the centre of the globe. Her hands were shaking with the effort of holding onto and directing so much power.

'Diminutus!' Jenn and Matt screamed together. 'Diminutus entirii'

Larena's body began to shrink. The light pulsated above their heads. Her cries grew fainter as her body withered. Jack and Helen both staggered to their feet. Huge pieces of brick and iron were now falling constantly around them. It was pure chance that they had not already been hit by something. But their luck would not last forever. Larena's form was now almost back to being the size of a raven. As she shrank, Auntie Jenn took two or three steps towards where she still hovered and spun in the air. With another cry of 'entirus captatii!' she threw the glass globe at Larena. With an ear-splitting crack the light in the globe went out and Uncle Matt leapt up to catch it before it could fall. Jack saw that the tiny figure of Larena, still in human form, was imprisoned inside it.

Helen had got to her feet. She stared with almost disbelieving joy at her parents.

'Mum! Dad!' she ran towards them, tears streaming down her face. The three of them stood hugging each other for a moment, oblivious to everything else.

Another deafening rumble sounded directly above their heads.

'Come on,' Jack yelled, 'run!'

They all scrambled along the passageway and into the outer atrium of the palace. Ahead of them were the iron gates. They were no obstacle now however, as both of them lay open, one twisted out of shape, the other hanging at a strange angle to the ground. Jumping over fallen boulders and rubble they raced towards the gates.

26

Reunions

Korellia was the first to see them run out of the collapsing building. Her eyes had been on the doors for some time while one of the young rebels tended the scratches from the talons of the blood bats. She cried out and pointed. Parenon had been talking to Orianna close by and they both turned as one and began running towards the children. Matt and Jenn both waved a signal that they were alright, but seemed relieved when the others came to give them supporting hands and shoulders.

Parenon grasped the globe containing the bird-sized Larena from out of Matt's hands. He glanced at him and uttered a single word. 'Larena?'

Matt nodded. Parenon threw his blue cloak over it.

'Let us keep her in the dark. At least for now. We cannot be complacent about one such as her. I believe she can still be capable of treachery.'

Jack turned and looked up at Orianna. He watched her for a few moments in silence as she turned aside and spoke to Parenon. Could the things that Jacques told him be true? Was he *really* her brother, Serrion Melgardes?

As he watched her, Parenon walked away and Orianna turned to look at him. She frowned as she saw the expression on his face and began to come towards him.

'Are you alright, Jack?'

What could he say? How could he begin? He couldn't

just go up to her and say 'I don't think I'm Jack Anders. I think I'm Serrion. You might be my sister.' He didn't know how to start, but he knew that he had to talk to her. All the others had to be told as well. Helen was convinced that what they had learnt in the dungeons of Atros was true. If he didn't say something himself, then she certainly would. He sighed. If he was going to tell them, he might as well start straight away.

Orianna repeated her question.

'Is everything alright?'

He looked up at her. 'Yes, yes thank you, I'm fine.' He said. 'But there's something I need to talk to you and Korellia about. Alone.'

They turned together and walked down the hill, away from the battle field, leaving the others behind them.

Three weeks had gone by. Their triumphant return to Beltheron had been saddened by the loss of so many friends. All such returns from war - victorious or otherwise - are saddened in this way. Amongst the cheering and waving crowds that greeted them on the streets of Beltheron, there were many who looked in vain for loved ones. They did not cheer but shed bitter tears instead. They sat alone in their homes that night and did not go to the feasts.

In those weeks, Jack and Helen told the council in great detail everything that they could remember about what Jacques Andresen had told them. Jack's parents, Peter and Sophie could still not be found anywhere. Many said that this was proof of their treachery, and that the story of Korellia's stolen baby was true. Harrow certainly seemed to take it seriously, and he spent many hours with Jack in deep conversation in his study at the top of his high tower.

On one such occasion, they were discussing what Jack

believed must have happened on that fateful day on Atros.

'Jacques cannot have survived.' Jack said. 'I didn't just *lock* him in that cell in the dungeons; I mangled the metal somehow with my power. There was no way that he could have got out. Helen and I both left straight away and it was only minutes later that the whole of that part of the palace collapsed. I am sure he didn't follow us out. He couldn't have done. There wasn't any time.'

Harrow nodded. 'Very well. I do not have your absolute faith that he could find no way to escape, but for now I am willing to accept it. In any case I am not sure that he can cause much evil without The Wild Lord to guide him. His hopes are at an end.'

It was time for Jack to return home to where he had been staying with Korellia and Orianna. They were delighted to be able to care for him. He was getting used to seeing the constant joy in Korellia's eyes now that she believed she had her long lost son with her again. Orianna couldn't do enough for him. These things were all great comforts. When he thought of all the changes he had gone through however, he still felt far from comfortable.

So, lost in his thoughts and anxieties, he ran down the stairs of Cleve Harrow's tower with no mind to the drop on his left or for his own safety. He hurried across the city, eager to get back to Korellia's house and the love he had missed in a family for so long.

He knew that he should feel grateful for this new life that had opened up for him, but his confusion about all the lies he had been told weighed heavily on his mind. He often found it difficult to sleep. He lay awake long into the night, turning over past events in his childhood. Jack felt tortured by memories of those he had believed and loved, and by the thought that none of it had been real.

One afternoon it all came gushing out. He had been

helping Orianna to clear away the kitchen when a plate slipped from his fingers and smashed on the floor. This little accident caused a burst of rage. He stormed out of the room, shouting and slamming doors behind him.

Orianna waited in the kitchen for a couple of minutes before following him to his room. She knocked gently on his door. There was no reply so she pushed it open and went in.

Jack was curled up on the bed. He didn't move as she walked across to him, but she heard a loud sniff and saw that his cheeks were wet. Orianna sat down next to him. She put her arm around him and waited patiently. Before too long, he began to speak.

'It's so hard to get used to it all, Orianna. I mean, I don't know where I belong, or what's real anymore. Here I am on a different *world*! I've found out that my whole life has been a lie.'

He sniffed again. 'What can I believe in now after everything that's happened? And what's next? Are you about to tell me that *you're* not real? That I've imagined everything? Sometimes I dream that this is all just some mad joke and Helen, and Mum, Dad and everyone else are going to jump through the door in a minute and shout 'Surprise!' I mean, what am I expected to think? On top of everything else, what about what Jacques told me. Is that true? I don't even know who I am anymore.'

He looked desperately at her. Orianna felt a pang of anguish for him, and frustration at not being able to help.

'I can hardly imagine what it must be like for you.' She said. 'But I *am* real, and so is Korellia. You are no longer Jack Anders to me. I *feel* in my heart that you are my brother, Serrion. With or without any proof I would be very, very proud to accept you as such.'

She hugged him tightly in her arms. She ruffled his

hair with her fingers, and bent to kiss the top of his head. Then Jack felt her hesitate for a moment. She gave a small gasp of surprise. Her hand moved to touch the back of his head again and she straightened up, pushing him to arms length so that they could look at each other.

Orianna was smiling down at him and an immense pleasure shone in her clear, bright eyes. 'I know that you're confused. Who wouldn't be? You say you don't know who you are or where you belong anymore, but just remember this. You haven't lost your parents; you have found your real family.' She continued very softly, 'if you still doubt me, here is your proof.'

Orianna held out her hands and helped him up off the bed. Together they walked to her room. She went to a wooden chest of drawers that stood against one wall. Orianna opened the top drawer and rummaged around for a brief moment. Jack tilted his head to try to see over her shoulder. What was she looking for?

She turned back to him, clutching a small hand mirror. 'Come over here' she beckoned to him. Jack walked towards her, still mystified. Touching his shoulder, she turned him around to face another mirror, a large, full-length one that stood on a wheeled frame in the corner of the room. As he stepped closer to it, Orianna moved behind him so that Jack could see both of their reflections looking back at him. Orianna raised the hand mirror behind him. After moving it backwards and forwards slightly, she found the right angle. There, suddenly reflected in the two mirrors, Jack could see the back of his own head. And in the middle, amongst all the dark brown hair, was a small but unmistakable patch of pure, pure white.

'I'm not Jack Anders,' he thought, with a sudden feeling of belonging. 'That is not my name anymore. I am Serrion Melgardes.'

Epilogue

Black clouds threatened the skies of Atros. Jagged lightning occasionally flared and lit up the horizon for a second or two, but all it showed was a still and barren landscape. No creature moved on the hard surface of the land. No bird flew under those heavy clouds.

Gendrell lay in ruins. It was at peace after its tortured history of cruelty. Neglect now claimed the city and had already started its long, slow destruction of Gretton Tur's domain.

It was dark and silent in his mighty castle. The candles had all burnt out. Cold wind blew through the cracked and gaping windows. It swept across the empty halls and down the murky corridors, occasionally rippling the torn drapes of curtains, and rustling the abandoned papers on the tables, blowing some of them onto the floor. Nothing else moved.

Down below, in the deepest of the dungeons, one cell door lay bent open. The twisted metal bars pointed out in sharp spikes. The cell, like the rest of the castle, was empty. Just outside these broken bars, on the floor of the dungeon passageway, a dark, round scorch mark had been burnt deep into the earth…

The End of 'The Beltheron Pathway'.
The adventure continues in 'The Beltheron Select' which will be published in 2009.